Her Christmas Cookie

WELCOME TO SEA PORT
BOOK FOUR

KATRINA JACKSON

Editor: A.K. Edits

Cover artist: Celia Moscote

Cover designer: Katrina Jackson

For all the people still looking for home.

Special thanks to Elisabet Salas for helping bring the Santos family to life.

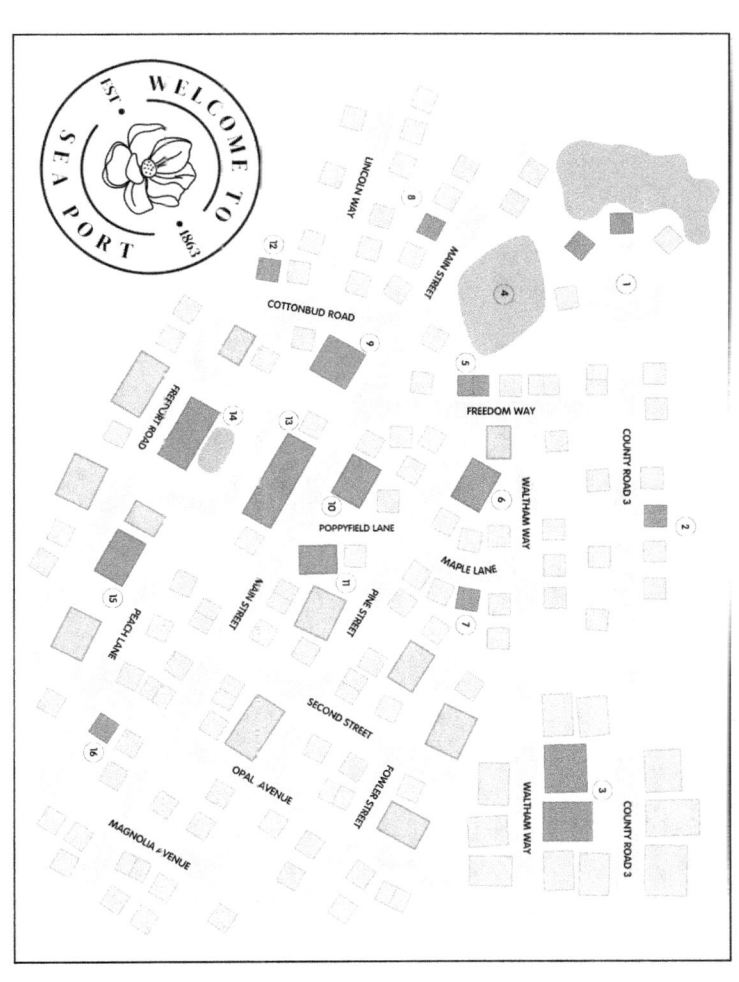

Map Legend

1. Perv Place
2. Santos's house
3. Freedom and Waltham farms
4. Douglass Park
5. Sully and Willie's duplex
6. Confections
7. Mary/Lorraine's cottage
8. The Grove
9. Knox's apartment
10. Sully's
11. Sunnyside Diner
12. Jonah's house
13. Sea Port Administrative Building*
14. Orange Grove County Library
15. La Bella Rosa
16. Bria's house

   *containing the Firehouse, Mayor's Office, Police Precinct, and Post Office

HAPPY HOLIDAYS FROM SEA PORT

Content Warnings

Homophobia
Allusions to child abuse
Abusive family dynamics

HAPPY HOLIDAYS FROM SEA PORT

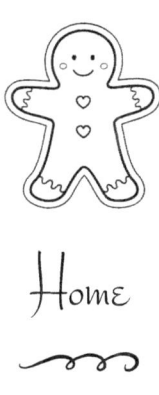

Home

~~~

SANTOS

This trip was Santos's idea. He broached the topic one night at dinner, his stomach all tied up in knots.

Mary had spent a late night prepping treats for a demanding septuagenarian's birthday. She came home with an empty stomach, tired feet, and a sore back. Santos and Knox had dinner on the table as soon as she walked through the front door. She'd plopped into a dining room chair, smiling gratefully before she started eating in silence, too exhausted to speak. Santos was always quiet, which left a vacuum Knox was all too happy to fill.

That night, Knox had a lot to say about some of the old farmhouses Jonah was renovating for new residents and all the paperwork that project required.

"If I make it outta this scheme without losing a finger to a papercut, I'll be lucky," he laughed into the silence.

Mary smiled in his direction but it was weak and hardly dislodged the exhaustion written all over her face. Knox brushed her cheek with the back of his knuckles and refilled her wine glass. She couldn't manage any small talk, but Santos could see the love in her eyes. It was their quietest dinner in a long time. Even Cat-leen was happily lounging under the table waiting for anyone, preferably Knox, to scratch her head, but Santos wasn't complaining. Mary plucked a small piece of chicken from her plate and offered it to Cat-leen, who'd greedily accepted before retreating under Knox's chair to snack.

Santos thought about waiting until Mary was less tired or Knox was less busy, but that could be months or years in the future. Sea Port was many things, but it hadn't been boring in a long while. And most importantly, he didn't want to put it off any longer. He didn't want them to run out of time.

Santos cleared his throat. Their attention focused on him and he shifted uncomfortably in his seat.

"I want you to meet my parents." The words were clipped and unnatural to his own ears — his voice almost never sounded like this anymore. Discomfort coursed through his veins.

"I've met your parents." Knox shrugged, smuggling more chicken under his chair to Cat-leen.

"What?" Mary said.

Santos cleared his throat.

"You need some more water, Marine?" Knox shot back, laughter bouncing around the edges of his words. Mary managed to laugh softly.

Santos took a reluctant but necessary sip of water before continuing. "I *said* I want you to meet my parents. Both of you. Officially as my...you know?"

"Partners," Mary offered at the same time as Knox said, "Roommates?"

Santos and Mary both glared at Knox.

"What?" Knox asked innocently. "The Santos family is very traditional. I just want to be clear."

Santos rolled his eyes. "My parents know about you." He glared across the table at Knox's shocked face. "*Both* of you," he clarified. "That's why I want you to meet them. It'll be like a formal introduction." His voice was thick with emotion even though he was trying to rein in his feelings.

"Formal, huh?" Knox asked, setting his fork down and leaning back in his chair.

Santos glanced in Mary's direction. She also set her fork down, but she was strangling her napkin in both hands as her gaze bounced back and forth between the men. He'd hoped this would be an easy invitation and acceptance. He even had a Google alert for flights to Denver in their budget. He was as prepared as he could be under the circumstances, but the silence that ate through the next few moments had Santos stressed.

Knox was staring at him with crossed arms and a blank face. Santos had lived with a delicious and, until very recently, forbidden desire to please Knox for his entire adult life and it was hard not to straighten his back under that gaze. But then Knox's mouth split into a bright grin. "Can you get your mom to make me some tamales?"

Santos's shoulders sagged forward and a small smile broke out on his mouth as he nodded excitedly. Well, excitedly for him. "She's gonna be making tamales all month long anyway, but I'm sure she'll make some special just for you two. If we visit."

Knox crossed his hands behind his head. "You had me at tamales. I'm in."

Santos hadn't expected Knox to put up a fuss, but it still felt good to have him on board. He took a deep breath before turning to Mary. She chewed at her bottom lip, still strangling that napkin in her hands, tearing it to shreds while she squirmed in her seat. The knots in Santos's gut tightened uncomfortably.

She forced a smile onto her face. "I'll think about it," she'd finally said. Her voice was bright, too high, fake, and then she'd pretended to have a headache and slipped away to shower.

"She said she'll think about it," Knox breathed. "So let her."

And he had. Sort of.

The next day, instead of asking Mary about the trip again, he talked to Knox about things he missed about Denver. And when Knox suggested they save money on their plane tickets and take a road trip, Santos had been all for it. And if they were driving out west, why not add stops to visit Knox's family? And Mary's? Mary's uneasiness about the trip had been proportional to Knox's excitement. Santos had felt torn between them.

He'd only wanted to discuss it with her, show her pictures, routes, budgets. Okay, he'd been desperate to convince her, nudging her until she lashed out. Santos had been terrified he'd ruined it all — not just their holiday plans but their entire relationship.

"You're being dramatic," Knox had sighed. Santos wanted to believe him, but Knox and Mary were the optimists, Santos was a realist, and surely nothing so good could last forever.

Knox had been right, of course.

Sure, it took Mary getting plastered for it to all come to a head, but if that was what it took to finally talk it out and stay together, that was all Santos cared about, even if they had to cancel the trip.

"We don't have to go," Santos whispered to a very hungover Mary.

He sat across from her at the table, worried he'd overwhelm her if he got too close. Knox was getting ready for work, moving around the kitchen, while Santos stared at Mary with an aching heart. Meanwhile, Mary was nibbling at a banana, looking skeptically at it after each bite as if she was worried she couldn't keep even that down.

"Calm down, Marine," Knox said with a firm hand on his shoulder. "Sweetheart, how about you tell us why you don't want to go."

Mary downed half a glass of orange juice. "I do want to go," she'd said weakly.

"Don't—" Santos started, but Knox squeezed his shoulder.

"I want to go," she said, her eyes pleading. "But what if your parents hate me?" Knox squeezed Santos's shoulder and just kept squeezing. "What if they don't approve of our relationship?"

"What if they do?" Knox asked gently.

Mary didn't have a response to that, so she shut her mouth and stared down at her plate. If Knox hadn't had an iron grip on his shoulder, Santos surely would've ruined the moment, rushing in as he always did to smooth their way.

"Is there something else you're worried about?" Knox asked. Mary nodded silently. "Do you want to share it with the class?" he chuckled.

Mary rolled her eyes but did smile, so that was something. "What if *my family* doesn't accept us?"

Santos wanted to lob Knox's question back at her, but he pressed his lips shut and waited for Knox's response, trusting him to know what to say when Santos didn't.

"Then they don't accept us and we move on with our lives," Knox breathed matter-of-factly.

"It's not that simple," Mary challenged.

"Yeah, it is. Or it can be if you let it."

Knox finally let Santos go and moved between them, looking down at them as if they were two hopeless souls. He checked his watch before turning his attention on Mary.

"We got a mortgage now," he said. "We're still paying off that California king mattress. If we ever get a minor league baseball team, we're buying season tickets. We have plans, and I'm not going anywhere just 'cause your great aunt whoever doesn't like me."

"It's my mom I'm worried about," Mary replied in a small voice.

"Her either," Knox said with even more force. "I'm not going anywhere. Period. How 'bout you, Santos?"

It took a few seconds for Santos to register the question, and when it sank in, he croaked out an answer. "Nowhere. This is home. You two are my home."

Mary's mouth lifted into a tentative smile.

"You hear that?" Knox asked Mary. She nodded, and he leaned forward, planting a kiss on her forehead. "Good.

'Cause I'd hate to have to fight you for custody of Cat-leen unnecessarily."

The cat in question meowed and pranced into the room. They turned to look at her, but she only had eyes for Knox.

"And I think you'd lose," Knox laughed, kneeling down to scratch her head. He checked his watch again and sighed. "Alright, I've got a meeting with the Mayor and a time off request to submit," he said, walking to the front door, Cat-leen prancing behind him to say goodbye.

"It can't wait?" Santos asked.

"Nope," Knox called, sitting on the bench they kept at the door to pull on his boots. "And I think you two need some time alone. To make up." He added that last sentence with a sly smile. When his boots were on, he scratched Cat-leen's head one more time and grabbed his backpack.

"You can send me pictures if you want. I wouldn't mind that at all," he said before pulling the door open and strutting outside.

Cat-leen hopped onto the bay window to watch him walk to his car and Santos watched her, nervous to be alone with Mary for the first time in their entire relationship.

"Are you still mad at me?" she whispered.

He shook his head quickly and looked her in the eyes. "I was never mad at you, just...overeager and frustrated."

"I felt the same. I love you."

Santos had never been happier or more relieved to hear those words. He leaned on the table and licked his lips. "You got time before work?"

"I think I might be a little drunk still."

Santos leaned back in his chair. "That's okay. You can just sleep, I—"

"Calm down, Marine," Mary whispered, and a shiver moved through Santos's body. "I'm just telling you so you can be gentle with me."

Santos's smile was so big it hurt. Well, big for him. He stood from his chair and walked around the table, offering his hand. "I always am."

Mary laughed at that. "Now, we both know that's a damn lie." A hiccup snipped her laughter out like a light, but not her joy. She let Santos help her from the chair and back to their bedroom.

"I think we should take some videos instead of pictures," Mary whispered as Santos closed their bedroom door behind them. "Knox would really like that."

And he did.

They started plotting their road trip over dinner the same night.

HAPPY HOLIDAYS FROM SEA PORT

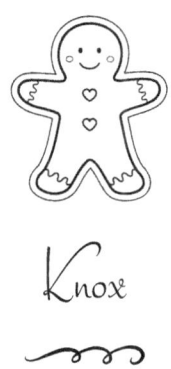

Knox

Knox woke up first. He didn't want to, but Mary was trying to bury her face into his neck — maybe even crawl under his skin — while Santos was doing the same from the back. It was sweet but hot as hell under their covers. He kicked the blankets from their tangle of limbs for some cool air, hoping that might encourage them to give him a sliver of space, but they inched closer instead.

He had to wonder if they didn't love him, or maybe they loved him a little too much; they were suffocating him either way. "You've gotta be fucking kidding me," he mumbled, shimmying onto his back.

Mary murmured something against Knox's neck. He couldn't understand a single thing she said, but he appreciated the little kiss at the end.

He had to strain his neck to peek at the bedside clock. They needed to be up and out of the house by nine, no later, and it was almost six. Knox would've loved another hour of sleep, but he was too damn hot. Since they didn't seem interested in giving him any space, he decided to make Santos and Mary drive while he napped in the back seat and stared up at the ceiling while he listened to the harmony of their soft snores.

Mary woke up soon after and snuggled closer like always, as if holding onto him would keep her dreams close. He'd never outright told her, but he loved when she did that. It nearly brought him to tears every time.

"You up?" she whispered, like a twenty-something boy with no social skills.

"No," Knox grumbled, a smile already lifting his mouth.

Mary kissed a path around his ear. "You wanna get up?"

Knox chuckled, deep and low. "On the way there, apparently," he said, feeling the first stirrings of his own arousal.

Mary tasted his throat in small sips. "Lemme help."

They spent the last week cleaning their house and packing their suitcases, with Mary giving them orders as if she'd been a drillmaster in her former life. They'd finally crawled into bed last night in a squeaky-clean house, overstuffed suitcases ready, too tired to be excited for the road trip to come. But now the trip was just a few hours away and Mary seemed hellbent on lifting their moods before the real fun began.

She shimmied down the bed and pushed his boxers over his hips. Her lips tasted every new patch of skin she uncovered while Knox stared at the ceiling, gasping at her touch. Knox moved to Sea Port with the hopes of building a life and he had. He was really going to miss this place.

"Fuck," he hissed as Mary slipped her mouth down his shaft. Knox closed his eyes and dug the back of his head into his pillow, groaning as she slowly started sucking him off.

Santos woke up when Knox's body tensed in his arms, sitting up in bed to get a better view. He rubbed his hand over Knox's chest, half-asleep but enjoying the show. Knox knew when Santos was awake for real when he heard the other man pull open the bedside table.

Knox opened his eyes just in time to watch Santos flip the cap on a small bottle of lube and cover his hard shaft with it. "Goddamn," he groaned, both because of the view and because Mary was opening her throat for him.

His muscles pulled tight and he started seeing spots as an orgasm built deep in his gut.

Santos started caressing Knox's chest again as his big, blunt fingers slipped through Knox's chest hair and tweaked the other man's nipples. Knox normally came quick in the mornings anyway, but this morning — with Mary sucking on the head of his dick, both their hands on his body, and the soft sound of Santos's fist on his own shaft mixing with Knox's own emotions about leaving their home — Knox came quick and hard.

And Mary drank his release down without missing a drop.

Knox was still breathing heavily when Mary crawled on top of him and guided his still-hard shaft inside her, grinding down on him before pushing Santos's hand out of the way so she could take his dick as well.

"Good morning," Santos groaned when he and Knox made accidental eye contact. Mary was writhing, moaning between them.

"Great morning," Knox corrected before sucking one of Mary's nipples into his mouth.

By the time they were showered, dressed, and almost ready to go, Mary was a bundle of nerves. Knox and Santos were packing the car while she sat on the porch, going over the Confections schedule one more time.

"It's not gonna fit," Santos said.

"That's what she said," Knox laughed.

"She's never said that," he mumbled, which only made Knox laugh harder.

"Ah, the magic of lubrication."

"Hey!" Mary called.

"It was a joke," Knox said like a chastened child.

Santos laughed under his breath.

Mary was wearing a pair of black leggings with one of Knox's oversized Marines t-shirts, her purse resting on the steps next to her.

"You going somewhere?"

"To the bakery. I need to go over a few things with Bria before we leave."

"I thought you already did that?" Santos sighed. Knox could hear the stress in his voice, still worried the wrong word might jeopardize their relationship.

"You runnin' away, sweetheart?" Knox asked lightly.

Mary rolled her eyes. "Running where? This town ain't

but this" — she snapped her fingers — "big. Where would I go?"

"Exactly," he purred.

She tried not to smile but lost. "I'll be gone ten minutes. Chill."

"Chill?" Knox laughed. "That's rich coming from you."

She blew them a kiss and then bounced down the last two steps. "And don't you forget it. I'll bring back some bagels for the road."

"And a chocolate muffin!" Santos called after her.

She waved her hand in the air. "And a chocolate muffin," she echoed.

They watched her walk down the street. Orange Grove County was one of the most beautiful places Knox had ever seen, but nothing beat the sight of Mary's ass on the move.

When he turned back to the car, Santos was still watching Mary's ass. "Tighten up," he laughed.

"That's what he said," Santos joked.

"It was funnier when I said it."

Santos finally tore his eyes away from Mary's retreating figure and cupped the back of Knox's head, pulling him close. "No, it wasn't."

Knox smiled as their lips touched. "Coward," he breathed against Santos's searching tongue. Santos grunted into his mouth. Knox knew the man wanted to tell him to shut up, but he was too busy sliding his tongue between Knox's lips.

Knox slipped his hands under the bottom of Santos's t-shirt.

"Hey!"

Santos's lips stopped moving and he groaned — not in a good way — into Knox's mouth.

"Excuse me," Lorraine squeaked and then cleared her throat.

"Hey, Lorraine, what's up?" they said, turning toward her eventually.

She shrugged happily. "Nothing much, just wanted to double-check y'all still want me to watch Cat-leen."

"We do," Santos called.

"We really appreciate you doin' this for us. Mary's nervous about leaving her."

"She hasn't been alone in three years," Santos added seriously.

"Which is why you're really doing us a solid," Knox sighed, poking his elbow into the other man's ribs.

Lorraine's eyes bounced between them before she let her gaze rest on Knox. "Sure thing. We're happy to help."

"We?" Knox asked.

"Oh, Jonah's gonna help," she said cheerily. "I will not be scooping a litter box."

Santos had a reputation for being a hard-ass before noon, but even he couldn't help but laugh at that.

"Does Jonah know?" Knox asked.

"He will eventually. Y'all have a good trip," Lorraine said and turned away, practically skipping across their shared lawn back to her and Jonah's house.

"I'm almost sad I won't be here to see his face when she springs that on him," Santos laughed.

"Damn shame," Knox said, scratching Santos's back. "Come on. Let's take everything out and start again."

"They won't all fit," Santos sighed.

"Yeah, they will," Knox replied, turning to Santos with a gleam in his eyes. "Have a little faith. This can be our first Christmas miracle."

Santos sucked his teeth, but the boyish smile Knox loved never left his face.

HAPPY HOLIDAYS FROM SEA PORT

Mary

Mary and Bria spent two weeks preparing for Mary's absence. They adjusted their baking schedule so Bria could handle it on her own. They reduced store hours to make things easier for Bria and Charlie to handle without her. Mary had even impressed Sal and Mrs. Wright for on-call duty just in case they got overwhelmed while she was away. Mary wasn't on board with promoting Bria to assistant manager just yet, but she didn't want her to fail either, so she'd stayed late the last few days to make a few extra batches of teacake and cookie dough for whenever Bria got stuck in the future. They were probably over-prepared, but that was better than the alternative. Someday very soon, Mary would need to hire at least one more cashier — maybe even a new part-time apprentice — but that would come after the road trip. After Mary had survived whatever emotional minefield this trip would hold.

She was ready to go. She was even a little excited — for two-thirds of the trip, at least — but this was the first time she'd left Sea Port since she'd opened for business and her anxiety was on high, mostly about leaving her babies, Cat-leen and Confections. Mary had spent most of yesterday alternating between cleaning, packing, and forcing Cat-leen to cuddle her, and now she needed to do the equivalent in the bakery.

"We went over this already," Bria sighed. She was leaning her hip against the prep table, one eye on Mary and the other on a batch of buttercream in the stand mixer.

Mary ignored her youthful nonchalance. "You need to be here for shipments. I love Charlie, but she's not getting up at five to meet the delivery truck. And we both know she won't bother going over the manifest as carefully as I need."

"I can literally hear you!" Charlie yelled from the store-front, where she was wiping down the display cases before opening.

"I forgot that was there," Mary muttered, glaring at the doorstop holding the swinging door open.

Bria turned away from her frosting to laugh loudly.

"I can hear you too!" Charlie yelled.

Mary moved to the door and smiled. "My bad. It's true, though." Charlie sucked her teeth and cut her eyes in Mary's direction. "But this way Bria can't convince you to cover deliveries just so she can spend a few more minutes in bed with her new girlfriend."

Bria choked on her laughter. "Can we not?"

Charlie skipped into the kitchen, her mood totally changed. "Oh nooo, let's. Let's shake the table for real."

"I hate it here," Bria sighed.

"Is it 'cause your girlfriend doesn't work here? Sounds a little codependent."

"What do you even know about codependency?" Bria spat back, rolling her eyes before shutting off the mixer.

"I know a lot about a lot of things," Charlie said, but then her face crumpled. "Well, I know *a little* about a lot of things."

"This is a place of work. How about we focus on that?"

"I can multitask," Charlie trilled.

Mary normally enjoyed watching Bria and Charlie fight — it was her main source of entertainment during long days at the bakery — but if she wasn't back home in the next few minutes, Santos would probably put out an APB to his little deputies to hunt her down. "Bria's right, let's stay on task."

Bria smirked at Charlie, who rolled her eyes and pretended to gag.

"We need to talk about the menu," Bria said, changing the subject. "You said you wanted to add another cookie?"

Charlie didn't care about product development unless there were samples for her to taste. "I'm out," she said, turning away at the first sign of baking even though she worked at a bakery.

"I've been working on a new sugar cookie recipe," Mary said, glancing down at the notebook in her hands.

"I know," Bria said excitedly. "They're great."

"They're okay." Mary frowned. "Something's not right, I just can't figure out what or why. I don't want to release them until they're perfect."

"They're literally the best sugar cookies I've ever had," Bria sighed, splitting the frosting into three separate tubs. She pushed one away, leaving it plain, and then started slowly dyeing the second tub, two drops of food dye at a time — much more careful than Mary ever was.

Now that Bria's attention was elsewhere, Mary took a deep breath. "You think it's good because you've never had my granddaddy Earl's sugar cookies. They're soft and buttery and a little spicy."

"Spicy?" Bria asked. "I don't remember that in the ones I've tasted."

"'Cause I don't know why they were spicy," Mary cried in dramatic anguish.

"Calm your tits, girl," Charlie called from the storefront, and Mary rolled her eyes at the kitchen door.

"I'm trying to get the base recipe down before I add a little nutmeg and a dash of pepper or whatever the hell he used."

Bria gave Mary a skeptical look over her shoulder while she folded the now-baby blue frosting until the dye was fully incorporated.

"Don't worry, you'll love them," Mary promised with a bright smile. It was always easier to reassure Bria than herself. "Grampa Earl's cookies used to melt in my mouth. It would've been nice if he'd just left the recipe for me instead of making me guess all these damn years, but that would've been too forward-thinking for him, I guess."

"Is this the same grandfather who taught you how to bake?" Bria asked.

"No, that was the other one. This is my maternal grandfather."

"What is it with your family and male bakers?"

"I don't know, actually. Most of the women in my family cook, but not many bake. And if they do, it's of the break-and-bake variety. *Maybe* a pie or two around the holidays, but that's it."

"But now there's you," Bria laughed.

Mary knew Bria meant it as a compliment, but those words made the knot of stress in her gut sink like a heavy weight. "And now there's me, trying to figure out this damn recipe all on my own."

"No one else in your family knows the recipe?"

Mary's smile wobbled a bit, but thankfully Bria had moved to the next tub of frosting, slowly folding red dye through the sugary goodness. "My grandfather taught my mother," she croaked out. "When I'm... When we get to California, I'm going to ask about it."

"Oh. Easy," Bria said naively.

"I wish. I've asked her before and she said no."

"Why?" Bria cried, shock written all over her face.

"You'd have to ask her," she sighed, remembering how much that rejection had hurt at the time. "My mother is... my mother. But I'm going to get it this time. I promise." Mary clutched her notebook to her chest, saying those last two words with conviction. She tried to reassure Bria and hype herself up at the same time, but she didn't feel any surer than she had a few moments ago.

"I believe in you." Bria finally said, turning back to her frosting.

"Thanks." She glanced at the clock with a sigh. "Okay, I'm leaving."

"Drive safe. Have fun. Good luck with your mom. Don't come back pregnant."

Mary's steps faltered at the kitchen door. Her mouth gaped open and she glared at Bria. "Why would you say that?"

"Have you seen you three?" Bria laughed. "'Cause I have and we've all been thinking it."

"All who?" Mary gasped.

"The whole town. But don't worry," Bria added. "We're all really excited about you three having the first Transplant baby."

"Don't call her that."

Bria's eyes went to Mary's stomach. "Her?"

Mary covered her stomach with her hands. "I didn't mean that. I'm not pregnant! Goodbye!"

"Not yet," Bria mumbled as Mary swept into the storefront, grabbing her box of treats for the road on the way.

She said goodbye to Charlie and unlocked the door for the morning crowd, slipping out as they filed inside.

She walked home with that ball of stress — not a baby! — still weighing her down. She didn't know what this trip would bring or what to expect of Santos and Knox's families. Unfortunately, she knew what to expect of her own, and she didn't know how to escape the fear of what was to come. But as she rounded the corner onto Perv Place — Knox and Santos's nickname for their little cul-de-sac — she told herself that everything would be alright and no matter what happened, she *would* return to Sea Port with Grampa Earl's sugar cookie recipe.

Come hell or high water.

I t was fucking Tetris, but Santos and Knox had finally gotten all their bags into the car and they were ready to go.

Mary was not.

She was sitting on the floor of their guest bedroom, which was really Cat-leen Cleaver's private space — the room where she went for uninterrupted naps when she got sick of napping in the living room or the master suite or on top of the dryer.

Knox and Santos were very respectful of Cat-leen Cleaver's privacy, waiting for her to seek out their affection. Mary was not, especially not today. They needed to get on the road and Mary didn't have time to wait for her cat to decide she wanted to see them once more before they left.

Their road trip didn't have firm dates, but Santos and Knox had cashed in all their PTO so they could be gone for up to a month — the longest time she'd ever been separated from Cat-leen since the day she'd adopted her. Mary hadn't been looking to adopt a cat, she'd simply wanted a little shot of dopamine at the animal shelter. But then she'd spotted Cat-leen, sitting sad and haughty in her cage, and next thing she knew, she had a cat in a carrier and a plastic bag of cat food to aid the transition. An impulsive decision, but not one Mary regretted. Not even when the cat had her sitting on the floor, trying to coax her from beneath the spare bed.

"Are you going to come out?" she asked in exasperation. She'd tried cheery, she'd tried angry, and she'd tried desperate, but of course, Cat-leen decided to entertain Mary's request when she sounded defeated.

One paw peeked out from under the bed, followed by another for a deep stretch, claws digging into the carpet.

Cat-leen's head appeared and she let out a little peep of a meow. Mary waited until she was fully out in the open before stroking her knuckles from Cat-leen's head down the length of her spine.

"Will you be good?" Mary asked, holding back tears. "Because you have to be good or else I'll be sad."

Cat-leen shook off her nap and her shiny black fur caught rays of sunshine filtering in through the window. She didn't answer, not a single meow or squeak. Typical.

"I'm going to miss you," Mary whispered as Cat-leen kneaded her claws into the carpet.

"All packed. Finally." Santos's big body took up the entire bedroom door, his expectant but patient eyes focused on her.

Mary smiled, even though she felt like crying. "Did you grab the bag with all of the presents?"

He started to nod but then shook his head before turning around and disappearing.

Mary turned her attention back to Cat-leen. "I'll be back before you know it. I promise."

Cat-leen had settled onto her stomach, her paws touching Mary's thigh. This was her moment. Mary quickly grabbed her cat and held her to her chest. Cat-leen howled and whined and then purred when Mary tickled the white patch of hair at the base of the cat's throat. She was nice when she wanted to be.

"Be good," Mary said, nuzzling her cat's nose. Cat-leen whined, growled for a second, and then started whining again.

"She won't be."

Mary looked up to find Knox leaning against the doorjamb, his body taking up the entire doorway. He aimed his softest smile at her as if she wasn't spiraling emotionally.

"She might be," Mary sighed defensively.

Knox shook his head and stepped into the room. When he was near, he squatted down and rubbed Cat-leen's head. Mary frowned as her anti-social cat started purring immediately, pressing her head into Knox's touch as if Mary hadn't all but birthed her into this world.

"She'll be mean and standoffish as usual. She'll nap in her favorite spots. She'll rip the shit out of the couch. And she'll be just fine."

Mary felt like she was losing the battle against her tears. "You promise?" she whispered sadly.

"I promise," he whispered. "And I'll make sure Jonah knows that I'll break every bone in his face if one of Cat-leen's whiskers even looks wrong when we get back."

"I love you. Please don't do that."

"I love you too," he replied, side-stepping her request entirely.

"We ready?" Santos yelled from the hallway.

Cat-leen stirred in Mary's arms. When Santos appeared in the doorway, he looked stressed. He'd planned this trip meticulously, including their departure time, and they were three minutes late, but when his eyes landed on them, his gaze softened.

"She'll be fine," Santos sighed gently.

"But what if she gets lonely?" This was Mary's fear. Cat-leen wasn't a social cat, but she'd grown accustomed to a house full of people who doted on her. Even with Jonah and Lorraine stopping by a few times a day, it wouldn't be the same.

Santos joined them by the bed, bending over and placing a hand at the nape of Knox's neck. "I texted Jonah earlier to look out for her. I also told him I'd break his legs if anything happened to her."

Knox laughed softly.

"Poor Jonah," Mary sighed, hugging Cat-leen close to her chest. "I told you they were quality guys."

"Quality?" Santos breathed.

"Not like the best men you've ever met?" Knox added.

Mary nuzzled Cat-leen's nose. "Men."

Cat-leen meowed in agreement.

HAPPY HOLIDAYS FROM SEA PORT

Lorraine

In winter, Lorraine usually sprinted to her car, drove five blocks to work, and then shuffled into the library exactly on time. She hadn't expected Sea Port to have an actual winter and that first cool gust of wind had given her a very rude awakening. If not for the fact that Jonah was folding her up like a pretzel every night, she might've left Sea Port at the first sign of morning frost without a second thought. But she was rolling with the punches of a Southern winter with Jonah's help — also known as his mouth — and a light jacket. Unfortunately, they'd had to cut their morning routine short so Lorraine could check on Cat-leen and Jonah could clean her litter box.

Lorraine had happily volunteered to take care of Cat-leen. She loved Mary, Knox, and Santos and she wanted to help them take this trip with ease. Jonah was also trying to convince her to get a dog, so Lorraine was using this as a trial run. If they could survive a few weeks taking care of Cat-leen, *maybe* they were ready for a dog. Maybe. They'd done well yesterday, hanging out with Cat-leen and raiding their neighbors' bar cart, but Jonah was making it hard to stay on task.

He trailed behind Lorraine across the lawn, his blunt fingers grabbing at her ass like a greedy child. They both knew he was strong enough to pick her up and carry her back to their house, but the horny whining was like an extended game of foreplay and Lorraine had nothing to complain about. They'd probably have enough time for a quickie since Cat-leen didn't seem fond of them and only wanted the fresh water and food they could provide; a stance Lorraine could support, honestly.

She was halfway across the lawn before Jonah grabbed her around the waist and pulled her back into his chest. He shoved his face into her neck and mumbled something she couldn't decipher but knew was probably filthy as hell. He tasted her skin and brushed his dick against her ass as they walked together. Lorraine giggled up a storm, already pushing her first meeting of the day back just a few minutes.

"Ain't nobody out here but us," he whispered against her ear. "I could lay you down right on this grass and eat your pussy and wouldn't nobody know."

"Jonah, you're a fool. Cut it out," she said, pulling away but giving his proposition some serious consideration as she walked onto Mary's porch — but only *after* they tended to Cat-leen.

Jonah waited at the bottom of the steps. "Come on, baby, just real quick before you head to work."

God, her pussy loved when he begged. "You said that two hours ago," Lorraine said giddily. "I'm probably going to be late for work messing around with you."

He jogged up the stairs. "You could be naked messing around with me right now."

"Keep begging and we'll see," she teased, fitting Mary's spare key into the front door. "It's just a scoop of food and some water. Maybe a little petting if she lets us."

She heard his heavy footsteps on the porch and then felt his arms wrap around her waist again. Jonah's hands moved from a conservative, if lustful, grip on her waist down her thighs. Instead of unlocking the door, she watched his hands move to the hem of her sweater dress. He pulled the fabric up her thighs, scraping his nails over her exposed skin while he sucked her earlobe into his mouth.

Lorraine moaned low and a little bit feral. She closed her eyes and enjoyed just how good Jonah always made her feel.

"Spread your legs, sweetheart," he whispered, the tips of his fingers teasing the seam of her thighs. Goosebumps erupted all over her skin as she granted his request. He slipped a hand between her legs, pressing her against their friends' front door.

"Oh god, this is so wrong," she moaned when his fingers brushed her bare clit.

"Shhh," Jonah hissed. "Damn, you're wet." His fingers smoothed down her folds and back again before he started circling her entrance.

"Keep doing what you're doing and I'll show you how wet I can get." Jonah grunted, and that was answer enough for what they both knew to be true.

Lorraine sighed in delight when he pushed two fingers inside her. Not that anyone ever asked her for dating advice, but if they had, she'd tell them to find a man who was good with his hands — personally and professionally.

It wasn't cunnilingus on the grass, but Jonah finger-fucking her slow and deep on the front porch proved that Perv Place was aptly named. Maybe one day, they'd petition the town to let them rename their little cul-de-sac officially, but for right now, this place was their little slice of heaven. Just close enough to downtown that they could walk to work if they wanted, but far enough away that the town gossip mill wasn't camping out on their front lawn, all in their business. Jonah moved his fingers inside her, pressing the heel of his palm against her clit, pushing deeper and deeper until Lorraine's knees started knocking together like maracas.

He fucked her until he had to hold her up while she came all over his fingers in the crisp morning sunshine. A beautiful morning indeed.

For a little while, at least.

Lorraine would've called it a comedy of errors except not a damn thing about the next few moments was funny. She was coming down from the high of her orgasm, her muscles spasming around Jonah's fingers, and all it took was one jerking movement of her hand on the unlocked door handle before their beautiful moment went to shit.

Her hand jerked, the doorknob turned, and the door creaked open. She made a mental note to have Jonah check on that later. It all seemed to happen in slow motion until Cat-leen Cleaver sprinted through the cracked door, down the front steps, and around the side yard. Jonah's arms were still wrapped around Lorraine's body as he spun them both around.

"Wait!" he cried, fingers still stuffed inside Lorraine.

She moaned and cried out at the same time, just as Cat-leen's dark body disappeared into the woods at the edge of Perv Place.

"No!" she and Jonah yelled futilely.

It took a second for them to disentangle their bodies and scramble down the porch, but Cat-leen was long gone by then.

"Fuck," Jonah spat, leading Lorraine after her.

"Mary is going to kill us," Lorraine cried, on the verge of tears.

"It'll be okay," Jonah said, slowing down for her to catch up. He tried to sound reassuring, but Lorraine wasn't in the mood.

She cut her eyes at him and swatted his hands away when he reached for her. "You don't touch me until we get that damn cat back," she said, stomping toward the trees.

"Wait," Jonah gasped, actually looking hurt. "Come on now, Raine. That's extreme. It was an accident! Let's talk about this."

She sucked her teeth. "We'll talk about it when she's safe and sound and not a second before."

HAPPY HOLIDAYS FROM SEA PORT

$\mathcal{D}$enver

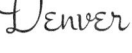

MARY

After three days driving from Sea Port to Denver, Mary had come to three rather important conclusions. First, Knox and Santos had the worst singing voices she'd ever heard. They were shaky and off-key; so far off key, she'd fantasized about flinging herself from the car just to be free of them. They had a whole boy band era karaoke session that lasted through all of Missouri and Mary had been extremely unhappy about it.

Second and most heartbreakingly, none of the budget motels they'd stayed at in a bid to keep this trip in budget had beds built for three. They pushed the beds together a few times, but after Knox almost fell through the crack one time, he banned them from doing that again. Some of the beds were bolted to the ground anyway. By the final stretch of their trip to Denver, everyone had stiff backs, cramped legs, and they were bitching and moaning at each other like never before.

Mary had never been more relieved than when they

finally made it to Denver. Relieved and a little lightheaded as well, but Santos had prepared them for the latter at least.

The third and most important thing Mary realized, as Santos maneuvered their car down the freeway, was that she had missed snow. Four dedicated seasons was half the reason Mary moved East for grad school. Technically Sea Port had a winter season, but seeing snow blanketing roofs as far as the eye could see had her missing a real winter, not the heavy rain and a thin layer of frost that passed for winter down South.

"I wanna make a snow angel," Mary whispered to herself.

"Hey, you awake?" Knox asked, reaching into the back seat to squeeze her knee.

"Yeah," she croaked. She tried to stretch, but her hands hit the roof as they had so many times over the last few days and she whined pathetically.

Knox squeezed her knee again. "Yeah, I know."

"We're almost there," Santos said, slowing the car in degrees. "You nervous?"

Santos lobbed the question to no one in particular, but Mary knew he meant it for her. He'd been treating her with kid gloves for weeks, which was unfortunate as hell because she missed him throwing her around in bed.

"I don't get nervous," Knox laughed.

"Only a little," Mary admitted.

Santos nodded but didn't respond. Mary noticed his jaw tighten, though, and based on the gentle squeeze Knox gave her, he'd seen it as well.

Santos said his family was fine with their relationship, but Mary didn't fully believe him. From everything she knew about Santos's family, she couldn't imagine they'd be okay with their son dating his best friend *and* the random baker they met in their small town, but she was hoping for the best.

Santos eased the car along the off-ramp and Mary leaned between the front seats to see what they could see. "This neighborhood's cute."

Santos simply grunted.

"It is," Knox said pointedly.

Santos grunted again.

They drove down streets with new-build houses that looked straight out of a big-budget holiday movie, uniform right on down to the styling of their Christmas decorations. The wide lawns were covered in thick blankets of snow with perfectly plowed sidewalks.

"Oh, I know these HOA fees are bigger than our mortgage," Knox joked. Santos and Mary nodded in unison.

After a while, the houses became smaller, older, built a little closer together, and covered in decorations that ranged from cheesy to extravagant to bordering on fire hazards, and Mary loved them all. She hadn't smiled so hard in at least two states.

A few moments later, Santos pulled into a driveway next to a house with an odd collection of colored lights slung across the roof and front porch, an inflatable team of reindeer on the roof, and a full nativity scene in the middle of the front yard.

"I love it," she whispered with a smile so big it hurt.

Santos turned the car off, and they sat in silence for a second before the front door flew open as if whoever was inside had been sitting at the front window, watching and waiting for their car to arrive. The porch light illuminated a small woman with medium brown skin in a long, black puffy coat clutched closed at her chest. Santos sighed and wrenched open the driver's side door. He yelled at the woman in Spanish. She stopped at the edge of her small porch and bounced excitedly as Santos climbed from the car.

"That's Santos's mom," Knox said.

"No shit," Mary laughed, unbuckling her seatbelt to get a better look. Santos stomped across the yard toward his mom. "I've never heard him speak Spanish before," she mused, slack-jawed.

"Hot as fuck, ain't it?"

Mary leaned over the front passenger seat to whisper to Knox. "This is terrible timing, but I'm hella horny right now."

"When have you ever been horny at an appropriate moment?" She punched him in the arm as he undid his seatbelt. "Stay there. I'll get your door," he laughed.

Mary turned her attention back to the porch while she waited. Santos and his mom were perfectly framed by the porch light and she gobbled up their reunion. His mother was holding his face and smiling up at him. Mary could feel the pressure of tears at the back of her eyes, but she blinked them away, refusing to miss a moment.

She'd been apprehensive about this trip for weeks, but seeing Santos in his mother's embrace wiped that feeling away. Whatever happened over the next few weeks, Mary knew all the hassle they'd endured thus far was worth it if it made him this happy.

Knox pulled her door open and offered his hand. She shivered at the cool gust of air he brought with him.

"Come on, sweetheart."

Mary's body was stiff after so many hours in the car. She leaned into Knox's side as they walked to the porch where they stood quietly, desperate not to interrupt Santos's homecoming. A tall man stepped onto the porch, followed by two younger but equally tall men — so obviously Santos's father and brothers that Mary's mouth fell open.

"This family's genes," she breathed.

Knox was standing behind her and bent down to whisper in her ear. "Between us and him, our kids are gonna be the prettiest babies Sea Port's ever seen."

Mary's eyes went wide and she turned to him. "Now when you say kids," she said, stressing the 's' at the end of the word. "How many tall, big-headed babies do you think I'm pushing out?"

He had the nerve to wink while not giving a numerical answer. They'd all been ducking and dodging around this topic for a good long while, but that couldn't last forever.

"Come in, come in!" Santos's mother called. When Mary turned back to the porch, Santos's entire family was staring at them. His parents' excitement at their eldest son's return was palpable. "Come in. It's cold. The boys will get your bags."

Santos's brothers sighed and stepped aside for their mom to lead everyone else into the house. Mary heard Santos mutter something in Spanish to his brothers, ruffling the hair of one, who ducked away from his hand but grinned happily.

"Come, come," Santos's father encouraged them inside with a smile and a friendly wave. "Welcome back, Billy."

"How you doing, Mr. Santos?"

Mr. Santos's face bunched together just like Santos's did when he was annoyed. "The cold aggravates my knees, but I try not to complain."

Mrs. Santos made a loud noise from inside the house and her husband ducked his head in embarrassment. "I might complain a little," he amended with a charming lift of his shoulders and a sly grin in Mary's direction.

"Ven. Let me get your coats," Santos's mother called, rushing them inside.

If not for Knox's hand at her back, Mary's feet might have frozen to the welcome mat, she was so nervous. But Knox pushed her forward while Santos extended his hand, both men helping her cross the threshold into the Santos home. There was something special about having their hands on her in that moment, but she also felt vulnerable at the same time.

The entryway was warm, cluttered, and adorably homey. Santos and Mr. Santos helped Mary and Knox with their coats and boots. When they were all squared away, Santos led them deeper into the house, following the sound of his mother's soft humming. She tried to take in all the décor — the big, plush, mismatched couches with colorful knitted throws over the back, the porcelain figurines on the fireplace mantel and coffee table, the pictures of Santos and his brothers through the years covering every wall. She could tell that these were the regular décor while the Christmas decorations were scattered amongst them — every flavor of snow globe imaginable, festive garlands and another nativity scene on the mantel, and so many tall candles scattered on nearly every surface around the room. It was exactly the kind of home

Mary had imagined Santos grew up in, but seeing it in person made her heart feel full.

They ended up in the kitchen where Santos immediately pushed up his sleeves and started washing dishes.

"Sit," his mother said in English, gesturing toward the kitchen table before switching back to Spanish when she spoke to Santos.

Knox pulled out a chair for Mary. She tried to take everything in, but she also couldn't take her eyes off Santos. They'd only just arrived and he was already helping his mother in the kitchen, laughing with her as they tried to get him to sit. The sight made something light and fluttery take root in her stomach. Knox somehow always knew what she was thinking and threw his arm over her shoulder, squeezing her close, and she leaned into his side.

She didn't know when, but Mary was definitely going to have their tall, big-headed kids.

"Are you hungry?" Santos asked.

"Huh?" Mary snapped, lifting her eyes from his ass.

"My mom made us dinner."

"Oh, she didn't have to," Mary started. Knox squeezed her shoulder.

"Too late." Santos said. "You hungry?"

"Starving, Mrs. Santos," Knox answered before Mary could object again.

"Good," Mrs. Santos said, beaming at Knox and Mary.

Mr. Santos stepped into the kitchen and pulled his son into a hug. Santos wrapped his arms around him, wet hands dripping onto the linoleum. His father kissed him on each cheek, whispering in Spanish as they held one another. Mary was trying not to cry, but she knew it was a losing game.

When they broke away, Mr. Santos's eyes were shining. His wife spoke in a voice that was hard and soft at the same time, but Mary couldn't understand a thing. She took French in high school and had never regretted that decision more than in that moment.

"We really need to get a Rosetta Stone," Knox whispered.

"I was just thinking that."

Santos stepped out of his parents' hold and moved next to Mary's chair. Mary held her breath as he introduced them in Spanish. She moved her gaze to the floor and studied the yellow cornflowers on the laminate tile rather than looking into Santos's parents' eyes too.

Santos switched to English. "Mamí, you know my boyfriend, Knox. And this is Mary, our girlfriend."

Mary knew Santos well enough to note the slight change in his voice. Instead of the flat affect he sometimes used with everyone else or the reluctant emotion she and Knox often had to pull from him, with his parents Santos's voice was deep, resonant, and full of pride. Mary lifted her eyes to look up at him and saw that he was as close to emotionally overcome as she'd ever seen him, and it pushed her closer to the same.

Mary's vision began to blur. She wiped at her eyes before she turned back to Santos's parents. His father's attention was on the three of them, but his mother's gaze was squarely on her — scrutinizing, but not harsh or uncomfortable. Not light, either. They waited in relative silence until Mrs. Santos decided to speak.

"I like the name Mary," she said carefully, in a heavy

accent like her husband's but deep and lyrical like her son's. "After the Virgin."

"Thank you, Mrs. Santos," Mary replied carefully. That's not who she was named after, but she for sure wasn't going to correct her.

She nodded once. "Call me Irma," she replied, stressing the first syllable of her name so it sounded like "ear-ma."

Mary burned that pronunciation into her brain but didn't use it so she didn't seem disrespectful. "Yes, ma'am."

Irma nodded again before raising one sharp eyebrow. "Y nietos? Bebés?" She was looking at Mary, but Santos translated even though this question seemed fairly clear, even for her.

"She's asking about kids. Mamá, we haven't—"

"Definitely," Mary interjected, cutting him off. They all knew it would happen, just not when. Irma didn't need to know all that, though. All she needed to know was that there would be grandkids, so Mary and her ovaries answered. "Definitely," she said again.

Irma nodded one more time before shifting her gaze to Knox. "I've been making tamales for days. I hope you're hungry."

Knox's entire face lit up. "Grandkids for tamales. Sounds like a fair trade to me." They all laughed, even Irma.

"Sit, sit, sit," she told Santos before turning to the stove.

Mr. Santos stepped forward with a smile. "Call me José," he whispered.

"You never told me to call you José," Knox laughed.

José shrugged. "You were never offering grandchildren before. You can start calling me José at the christening."

47

"Papá," Santos sighed in an exasperated tone as he put a pile of plates on the table.

"Qué? Queremos nietos, ahora. And your brothers can't keep girlfriends for more than a few months."

"We can hear you!" one of Santos's brothers called from the living room.

Irma yelled back. All Mary understood was the first word, "Bueno." She inferred the rest from tone and covered her mouth to giggle.

When his brothers walked into the kitchen, they were red-faced from the cold and maybe from being told off as well.

"Mary, these are my brothers, Francisco and Juan."

"Nice to meet you," Francisco said mildly.

Juan leaned forward with wide eyes. "So, are you three..."

But José cut them off. "Yes, together. We've already covered that. Go wash your hands."

"You mean we missed it?" Francisco whined.

"Sì," Irma answered in a light trill as she put a platter of tamales on the table in front of them.

"You sent us out to get their bags on purpose, didn't you?" Juan asked.

"Sì," Irma said again, a small smile spreading across her face. She piled three tamales on Mary's plate with a bright smile. Mary got the message: one tamale for her and two tamales for their future babies.

Santos sighed as Knox doubled over in laughter.

This wasn't at all how Mary thought this introduction would go, but she was pleasantly surprised.

HAPPY HOLIDAYS FROM SEA PORT

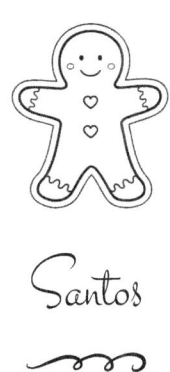

Santos

His parents' house smelled exactly like he remembered and Santos was trying not to let it bring him to tears. He'd of course been homesick every now and then while living in Sea Port, but he'd spent his entire adult life missing home and had learned to compartmentalize it well. But their kitchen smelled like tamales and toasted spices and he finally felt like home.

They'd made some changes since he'd been gone. His dad had finally repainted the living room — at least Santos thought the paint was fresh under all the family pictures — the dishwasher was new, and the refrigerator was bigger; small changes Santos knew made his mother happy, which made his father happy in return. For the most part, the house was exactly as Santos remembered, but he was seeing everything through new eyes with Mary and Knox by his side. He wanted them to love his family and their house as much as he did, so he took every smile, every peal of laughter, and every tamale Knox happily accepted from his mother as a good sign — a hopeful sign Santos held onto with both hands.

"Here's the basement," Francisco sighed, leading them downstairs into the laundry room that served as a neutral zone between the rest of the house and the bedroom his dad and uncles had built.

Francisco's voice was dripping with annoyance and Santos turned around, preparing himself to see something on his brother's face that might change their relationship forever. Instead, he just saw his little brother's petty bullshit — the same shit they'd been fighting about for most of their lives.

"My room," Francisco bit out, rolling his eyes.

"It was mine first," Santos reminded him.

"Whatever," Francisco said. "Just don't break any of my stuff."

The instinct to argue with his brother was baked into Santos's DNA, but his eyes landed on Knox and Mary, standing in front of the washer and dryer, eyes on the concrete floor while they tried not to laugh or get caught in the fray. Their presence was the only thing that saved Francisco from Santos escalating their fight. This time.

"Hey!" Santos called to his little brother.

Francisco was already halfway up the stairs, but he took two steps back and bent down to glare through the banister. "What?"

Santos glared back. "I missed you, Paco."

Paco rolled his eyes again. "Yeah, yeah. I missed you too." He tried to hide his smile and failed, and as always, it was infectious. He stood straight and started making his way upstairs. "Don't break my bed, hermano," he laughed, disappearing upstairs.

Santos cursed at him in Spanish but he was long gone. Mary and Knox were barely keeping it together, covering their mouths to hide more laughter. Santos pursed his lips and turned toward the bedroom door. "Come on."

The room looked more or less the same as when Santos had lived here, even with Francisco's knickknacks scattered around — framed baseball cards he'd been collecting for most of his life, posters of his favorite rappers, and far too many DVDs stacked neatly in bookshelves. Not a book in sight. His brothers had brought all their bags down here before dinner and pushed them against a far wall.

"Oh, thank god," Mary sighed, pushing past Santos and starfishing on the queen-sized bed.

"I kinda thought your parents would put us all in different rooms," Knox laughed, looking around the space.

"My mom turned my old bedroom into her sewing room a year after I enlisted. She's not moving her things for me or anyone. I guess she could've put Mary there, but..."

"Defeats the purpose if you two were gonna be down here fucking anyway," Mary laughed.

Knox chuckled softly. "We wouldn't dare." Santos reared back, offended, which made Knox laugh harder. "Or maybe we would."

Santos grunted. He'd never once had sex in his parents' house, but if he'd known Knox thought they wouldn't have sex the *entire* time they were here, he might not have pushed so hard for this visit.

Mary moved her arms above her head. "Guess the hope for

grandkids overruled it all," she sighed. Her t-shirt rode up her body, exposing her soft stomach. It had been a long trip with lots of hours stuck in their car and sleeping in lumpy beds, but not nearly enough privacy or time to relax. They were all tired.

But not *that* tired.

Knox walked back to the door and pushed it shut. "Oh, it locks," he said giddily.

"You up for this?" Santos asked, his fingers already pulling his jeans open.

Mary cracked one eye open just as Knox moved to Santos's side. "Always," she whispered.

Knox ripped his t-shirt over his head. "Me three," he said, climbing onto the bed. He shoved his face into Mary's stomach and kissed her skin. Mary's laughter filled the room as Santos pushed his zipper open and Knox shoved his head under her shirt.

It had been far too long since they got to be together the way they liked and Santos felt a lightness in his chest. His old bed would be a tight squeeze, but they could absolutely make it work. They always worked so well together.

Santos was just about to climb onto the bed when there was a quick knock on the door. Mary sat up on her elbows and Knox lifted her shirt with a guilty look on his face.

"Yeah?" Santos called.

"I forgot my phone charger," Francisco yelled from the laundry room.

Santos rolled his eyes and pulled his zipper up. He waited for Knox to reluctantly pull his head out from under Mary's shirt and they sat next to one another like they were in trouble. Santos unlocked the door and pulled it open, sighing in frustration. Paco's gaze bounced around the room as if he'd expected them to be in an orgy in the two minutes they'd been alone. Maybe if he'd been gone for five minutes, but two was a bit much.

They were all completely silent as Paco bent down next to the bedside table and pulled the charging block from the wall.

"Anything else?" Santos asked.

Paco hesitated for a second but then shook his head and continued from the room with a bright red face as if the reality of their relationship had finally dawned on him. Santos smirked and bit back a laugh until he pushed the door closed and locked it again.

Knox broke first. "Poor Paco," he laughed.

"He seems innocent," Mary said.

Santos rolled his eyes. "He broke my PlayStation when he was ten. He's not that innocent."

Knox covered his face and laughed so hard he started wheezing.

Mary leaned back on her palms. "The teasing older brother thing is sexy," she said, spreading her knees.

Santos stepped between her legs. "How sexy?"

Mary's tongue ran over her bottom lip and she moved her hands to his zipper, pulling it down with deliberate care.

"He asked you a question," Knox whispered.

"I was about to show him," Mary teased, moving her hand over Santos's groin. He just managed to swallow his groan. "And then I'll show you."

Knox brushed his mouth over hers. "Good girl."

She reached into Santos's pants while Knox stood, cradling the back of Santos's head as they locked eyes. They stared at one another while Mary pushed Santos's pants and underwear down to his knees. There were only a few inches between them, but that was too much. Santos reached out and wrapped his arm around Knox's waist, pulling him close.

Knox cupped Santos's cheeks with his palms. "This what you wanted?"

Santos grunted as Mary's wet tongue tasted the length of his shaft. He carefully dug his free hand into her soft curls while she sucked the head of his dick between her lips.

Knox's mouth was so close but he wouldn't kiss him. Every time he moved closer, Knox leaned away, watching him with a love-drunk look on his face. "Is this what you wanted? To get me and Mary in your parents' house so we could get her pregnant?"

Mary grunted, and because the head of Santos's dick was sitting at the opening of her throat, he jumped, groaned, and tightened his hold on the two people he loved with his entire soul. Her greedy lips and tongue tasted every inch of his shaft.

"You wanna keep her full of come and then send her upstairs to play happy family with the in-laws?"

Mary gagged a little and pulled back. Cool air hit Santos's wet shaft. She was panting, lips wet, a bit of drool on her chin.

"You okay?" Knox asked.

She nodded quickly. "Sorry. Didn't expect that."

"Expect what? This ain't your first time sucking his dick."

Mary shook her head. "No, the keeping me full of come part. I like that. Keep going," she said in soft breaths before opening her mouth wide and getting back to work.

Santos groaned loudly and his head fell back. Knox watched Mary suck him deep and slow for a few seconds before he turned Santos's face back to him. Santos tried to kiss him again and cursed when Knox pulled away.

"Or do you want me to suck your come out of her pussy every time?"

Mary squeaked and shoved her face further down his shaft until he could feel her nose in his pubic hair.

"Fuck. Fuck," Santos groaned. His voice was full of pleading, wanting, desperation.

Still, Knox wouldn't kiss him. "That what you want?" Santos nodded quickly and Knox leaned close. "If that's what you want, then I wanna hear you say it."

Mary hummed appreciatively while the sound of her sucking filled the room.

"Yes," Santos groaned. "I want all of that."

He leaned close. Their lips touched. "Good boy," he whispered before feeding his tongue between Santos's lips.

MARY

Mary wanted to sleep in more than life itself but she woke up bright and early, happily sandwiched between Santos and Knox. She basked in the feeling of a good night's sleep for a few moments before she accepted that she wouldn't be getting back to sleep anytime soon.

She slithered down the bed — something she'd become adept at in the past year and a half — and rummaged around in her suitcase for clothes. The room was comfortable but chillier than Mary had grown accustomed to in the South. Even though Santos and Knox were mad about her over-packing, she found a fluffy robe in her suitcase and didn't regret a thing.

She unlocked the bedroom door with her toiletries in one hand and walked to the other side of the laundry room to the bathroom. After days of budget traveling, Mary sighed audibly under the strong pressure and water hotter than she could stand. She couldn't tell if she was in pain from the long hours in the car or last night, but either way, her sore muscles appreciated that shower more than any she'd taken in recent memory.

If she'd been home, she'd have stayed in the shower until the hot water ran out, but she was raised better than that. Once she was clean and dry, she wrapped her terrycloth robe around her and took her sweet time getting ready, which meant putting on a face mask and checking her texts. The first message was from Lorraine.

> Hey! How's the trip going?
>
> Are you in Denver?
>
> Are his brothers hot?
>
> If yes, are they single?
>
> Gay? Straight? Queer? Open?
>
> Asking for friends.
>
> Named DeJuan and Charlie.

. . .

Mary smiled to herself, missing home and the messy, meddling friend duo Lorraine and Charlie had become. Charlie expressed her friendship by sharing a little of her gossip cache while Lorraine, Mary had discovered, demonstrated her affection through ill-advised matchmaking. DeJuan had managed to dodge most of Lorraine's efforts by not living in Sea Port and being — so far as Mary could tell from her stories — constantly moving from glamorous city to glamorous city being...glamorous. But Charlie was right there in Confections almost every time Lorraine dropped in for her daily sugar fix, giving Lorraine lots of time to make finding Charlie a man her personal mission. If not for the extremely limited population of young, single people in Sea Port, Lorraine would have had Charlie on a date every other day, but she was undeterred. Clearly.

Lorraine's frustration at Sea Port's population deficiencies had only grown as she'd settled into her life there. The lack of dateable youngsters was even starting to affect her relationship with Mayor Waltham in the run-up to the next mayoral election, but that conflict was officially none of Mary's business. She was on vacation and planned to leave Sea Port business in Sea Port — unless it had to do with her bakery.

Made it to Denver.

Santos family is adorable as fuck.

I'm his mother's fave because my uterus is in working order.

> Brothers fine as hell. Will investigate for the single ladies of Sea Port and DeJuan.

> How's my girl!? Give her extra treats for me!!

She skimmed through the rest of her messages, updating her friends as necessary. But then Mary saw her mother's name and it wiped the smile from her face.

> How's my grandcat?

It was such an innocuous question — kind, even — but it made Mary's stomach clench in anxiety. Every message Mary exchanged with her mother was somehow layered with unmet expectations and resentment. Mary had grown tired of her mother's refusal to acknowledge her life in Sea Port. She didn't ask about Confections, she didn't ask about Knox or Santos, she didn't even ask about the weather, only Catleen. Over the years, Mary had learned it was best to match her mother's energy, so she asked about her mother's favorite tv show rather than her parents' recent separation. They checked in with one another regularly, never really sharing anything important, but Mary knew they couldn't dance around their real lives forever.

While Santos and Knox had been happily planning their portions of the road trip, Mary had planned hers with veins full of dread. Sure, she'd done the most important thing, finding them a place to stay, but she still needed to tell her mother and she was running out of time. If they stuck to Santos's travel schedule, they'd be in her hometown in two weeks. Even if they stayed a few extra days in Denver or Vegas, their plan was to reach California by Christmas Eve and knowing Santos and Knox, they would.

Maybe it was the good night's sleep, maybe it was the even better sex, or maybe it was the scalding shower, but Mary finally decided to just pull the Band-Aid off. Her fingers flew over her phone screen and she pressed send without a second glance. She needed to get this done quickly or she never would.

> Mama, I'm coming home for a short visit.
>
> I'm driving so I'm not sure when I'll arrive. Two weeks max.
>
> We're staying at Dom's.
>
> I'll let you know when I'm there.

Once the message had been delivered, she chewed the inside of her cheek, realized her error, and started typing again.

> By 'we' I mean my boyfriends.
>
> Two of them.
>
> We've been together for over a year.
>
> They want to meet you.
>
> Cat-leen is great.

My friend is cat-sitting while we're traveling.

S he couldn't look over her messages again. She was tired. Texting her mother made Mary feel like she'd sprinted a mile and she had nothing left to give her today, so she muted the conversation and put on a podcast to take her mind off things.

She lifted her eyes to the mirror and forced a smile onto her face. "Baby steps," she breathed at her reflection. "We're perfect as we are."

When she walked back into the bedroom, Santos and Knox were still asleep. In her absence, they'd scooted toward the middle of the bed. One of Knox's arms was wrapped around Santos's waist. It was so beautiful she wanted to cry. She also wanted to rip her clothes off and crawl back into bed with them. She resisted the urge, but only because her mind was still troubled by thoughts of her mother. Instead of drowning her anxieties in sex, Mary dressed quickly and ventured upstairs in search of coffee, breakfast, and pictures of Santos as a baby.

When she stepped through the basement door, the sounds and smells of the Santos household hit her in a warm wave — loud Spanish music and strong coffee welcomed Mary into a new day. But the best part of it all was that she hadn't heard any of this before, which meant the basement was very well-insulated. It was too late to change her muffled screams from last night, but tonight was a brand-new chance to scream louder.

Mary followed the coffee and music to the living room, where she found Mr. and Mrs. Santos in matching Marines sweatsuits. They'd pushed the coffee table to the side in front of the TV and were following a low-impact cardio workout on the screen. Irma's long, gray-streaked black hair was tied in a loose braid down her back and José had a small towel thrown over his right shoulder, picking it up every few steps to wipe at his damp forehead. It was hands down the cutest thing Mary had ever seen.

"Good morning, Mary," Irma called without interrupting her knee lifts and torso twists.

"Good morning," José said, immediately stepping in her direction.

His wife's voice stopped him. "The workout is not over, mi amor," Irma trilled menacingly. It was the sweetest threat Mary'd ever heard. José sighed resignedly and got back to their workout.

"There's coffee in the kitchen," Irma called, transitioning to front knee lifts. "Help yourself. We'll be done soon."

"Soon," José scoffed.

"Thank you," Mary said, stepping around them.

She really liked Irma. She'd of course *wanted* to like Santos's mom, she'd just never thought the woman would like her. In the kitchen, she poured a mug of coffee, feeling embarrassed she hadn't even considered learning a little Spanish beforehand. She knew Santos's parents were only speaking English for her and she didn't love that feeling, so she sipped her coffee while searching for online language courses. The next time they came to visit Santos's family, she wanted to at least be able to speak a few words.

She also wanted Santos to talk dirty to them in Spanish, but he'd only do that if they could understand his commands.

About ten minutes later, Santos's parents finished their workout and Irma walked into the kitchen, patting her damp face with the towel. "Are you hungry?" she asked.

"Oh no," Mary said, jumping up from the kitchen table. "Coffee's fine. And you don't have to wait on me, especially not after your workout."

Irma gestured for Mary to sit and turned to the refrigerator, ignoring her without a word.

Mary's fingers twitched in discomfort. "Can I help you at least?"

Irma made a slight clucking noise in the back of her throat — a noise Mary recognized from her interactions with every older brown woman she'd ever met. It meant: "No, and how dare you ask?"

Irma pulled eggs and tortillas and other ingredients from the refrigerator.

"Does Miguel like this breakfast?" Mary asked, even though Santos's real name sounded odd on her tongue.

Irma shook her head. "No, Miguelito hates breakfast." She smiled fondly as she cracked one egg after another.

"Okay, good. I wasn't sure if that was because of me."

"No. He's always been this way. Even when he was a boy. Juice, water, *maybe* a banana, but nothing else."

"He's not picky with food when he does eat, though," Mary said, feeling a foolish need to defend him, even to his mother. She also inched closer, coffee cup clutched in her hands. She didn't normally get to watch other people cook, but she'd loved it since she was a girl.

"No," Irma laughed. "He is not picky. When he was little, he was the fattest baby. His cousins still call him Gordito."

"Um..."

"Little fat boy," Irma said. "He was perfect. Big belly, fat legs, big cheeks. He loved my pan dulce, all the sweet cookies and cakes I would make. But only mine. I used to send him packages of sweets when he was in the Marines."

Mary lifted her eyebrows and tried to keep her voice calm. "You do know I'm a baker, right?"

Irma was tending to a frying pan of eggs when her hands stopped. She turned to Mary and it looked like there were lights dancing in her eyes. They stared at one another for a long moment before Mrs. Santos let out a laugh from deep in her gut. The sound was elegant and high-pitched. For a second, Mary wondered how stoic Santos had come from this woman, but then the laughter faded and she fixed Mary with a serious stare. Yeah, she could see the family resemblance.

"He has fallen in love with a baker and a Marine. Of course, he has. His brothers will never stop teasing him when they understand."

They laughed together for the first time. Mary hoped it wouldn't be the last.

"Do you know how to make conchas, Mary?"

"I don't even know what they are." Her head turned slightly at the sound of one of Santos's brothers running down the stairs.

"Mamá," he called.

Irma called back in Spanish before she turned back to Mary. "They're Miguel's favorite. I will teach you."

"I'd love that," Mary said excitedly.

"Good. And then we can talk wedding dresses."

"Oh my," Mary breathed.

HAPPY HOLIDAYS FROM SEA PORT

Knox

Knox blinked awake in the dark basement. Mary was cuddled up against his side, her face pressed against his shoulders, her soft breath keeping pace with his own. He couldn't have moved without waking her up, so he didn't. Santos was on her other side with a stranglehold on his pillow. His snores were not soft, but Knox found them comforting still. It wasn't the same as being back in their bed at home, but it was close.

Christmas was still a ways away, but the Santos family had decided to move some of their Christmas celebrations up since all their sons were in one place again. This had inspired one of many fights among the brothers, with Paco and Juan grumbling about the family bending over backward for their golden child while Santos chalked it all up to his family looking for any reason to throw a party. By that point, Knox and Mary had become comfortable with their roles as spectators and waited patiently for Irma to rein her sons in. Knox was excited about getting on with the rest of their trip, but leaving the Santos home did make him sad. The Santos family was exactly what he used to daydream about as a kid. He was going to miss them all, even Paco.

Santos rolled onto his back with a groan.

"Shh," Knox hissed, carefully wrapping his arm around Mary's back as if he could protect the last bit of her sleep with his arm.

"Sorry," he whispered, a little too loud for Knox's liking. "Shh."

Santos threw his body around Mary's back and kissed Knox's forearm before resting his cheek on the same patch of skin. "What are you overthinking about?" Santos asked, his voice rough with sleep.

"Shh," Knox whispered, shifting in bed as his dick stirred.

"Answer the question."

"Christmas."

The room was silent for a few seconds before Santos sighed heavily. "Give me a real answer or I'm gonna wake Mary up and let her ask you."

"It's too early in the morning for all this," Knox sighed.

Even Santos's laughter was sexy as fuck.

Knox rolled his eyes and thought about arguing, but Mary was miraculously still asleep between them and he didn't want to wake her. Besides, Santos had started kissing Knox's forearm again as he snuggled closer to Mary.

Knox stared up at the ceiling, blinking in the dark before he started speaking, reluctantly at first.

"Sometimes my parents tried to pretend like they had

their shit together, usually around the holidays. I don't know why 'cause they really didn't celebrate — no decorations, no Christmas trees, not even a good meal on Thanksgiving. But if it had been a good year..." He stopped, grasping for the right words to describe his fucked up childhood.

He hadn't thought about his parents in months, even longer since he'd felt compelled to speak about them, and a lifetime since he'd seen them. Santos and Mary knew enough about Knox's childhood to never ask about his family because *they* were his family.

"If it had been a good year, my dad would take all the money they had in their bank account and get a Boston Market family dinner for Christmas. If I was lucky, I could eat my whole meal before they started fighting with each other. Usually about how much the food cost."

Santos moved his left hand to Knox's stomach and his abs jumped. He snatched his hand back a few centimeters and waited nervously. Knox could feel the heat of Santos's palm hovering just above his belly button; his heart was racing. He worried that maybe he should've lied.

Then Mary obliviously shifted between them, pressing her cheek against Knox's chest, right over his heart, and Knox exhaled loudly. Santos slowly lowered his hand back to Knox's stomach, but his touch was hesitant, just resting on the surface as if he was ready to snatch it back at any moment. Knox pulled his right hand from behind his head and carefully covered Santos's hand with his, pressing it against his stomach, caressing Santos's skin.

"I was thinking how I've never really had any holiday

traditions I wanted to pass down to someone, but I want some. That's all."

Santos shimmied up the bed, his body dragging against Mary's sleeping form. She mewled softly into Knox's chest. He pressed his face into the crook of Knox's neck and kissed the delicate skin where his pulse was running wild laps through his veins.

"You can have mine," Santos whispered in Knox's ear. "You can have my family traditions. We can make some for just us. Whatever you want."

It wasn't the words that hit Knox right in the chest, it was the way he said them. All the emotion in Santos's normally flat tone. The heat of those declarations on Knox's skin. The way he could feel Santos's and Mary's love covering every inch of him.

"Okay," Knox whispered. He didn't feel strong enough to say anything else because there weren't enough words to describe how he felt.

MARY

M ary woke up in the middle of their conversation, her second-favorite way to see another morning.

She was getting used to the Santos basement. It wasn't home, but as long as they were tangled together, Mary was happy.

"So there's not gonna be eggnog?" Knox asked. His words rumbled against her ear. She loved his voice any time of the day, but first thing in the morning and late at night were the best.

"No eggnog," Santos confirmed. "There'll be rompope, it's about the same. Although I can go out and get you eggnog if you want."

"Nah, that's okay."

"If it makes you feel any better, my Tio Hector will put as much rum in your champurrado as you want. Oh, and there'll be tequila. So much tequila."

"What's champurrado again?" Knox asked, stuttering adorably over the word.

"Like hot chocolate," Santos said, actual excitement lifting his voice.

"I love hot chocolate," Mary interjected, her voice still hoarse with sleep.

Knox laughed softly as if he didn't want to disturb her place on top of him. Santos pressed his face into the crook of her neck, breathing her in. He kissed her gently just behind her ear, his favorite way to say good morning. "We both do," he whispered, grinding his hips into her ass.

"Jesus," Knox laughed.

Santos was pressing his semi-hard dick against her ass and she was just about to spread her legs for him when there was a knock on the bedroom door.

"What?" Santos yelled, frustrated.

Mary recognized the voice on the other side as Juan's, but he was speaking in Spanish and she couldn't understand a word. She tightened her arms around Knox and pressed her cheek against his chest, listening to his gentle gallop of a heartbeat. After a quick exchange, they heard Juan's footsteps retreating through the laundry room.

"My family's on their way. We should get ready." He sounded sad and excited at the same time.

Mary reached back to pat his cheek. "We can shower together," she offered to lift his mood. It lifted something.

"Water conservation is really important," Knox said, already pushing the covers from their bodies. "Let's go."

Santos pulled the covers back, his excitement as palpable as Knox's. A perfect way to start the day.

Santos led them upstairs. He was holding a thick, red envelope behind his back. She could feel the nerves rolling off him. He was so adorable.

Knox extended an arm around Mary to squeeze Santos's shoulder just before they walked into the living room. Paco and Juan were sitting on the couch, their attention shifting from the television to their phones and back again. Only Juan acknowledged their presence with a murmured, "Good morning." If Irma had been there, she might've yelled at them for not making room for their guests, but Mary was excited they didn't see her like a guest anymore.

"Where's mamí?" Santos asked.

Juan tilted his head backward, so Knox walked off in that direction.

"Where's papá?" Santos asked.

"Garage," Francisco mumbled, sounding irritated.

"I'll go get him," Santos told Mary. She nodded and watched him leave the room. The younger Santos brothers looked at one another and then turned to Mary.

"Fuck, are you pregnant?" Paco groaned.

Juan sucked his teeth. "Shit. We pooled our money to get mamá a necklace. If you give her a grandkid, she won't even care. Please don't be pregnant."

This was hands down the most either brother had spoken to her since she'd arrived. Of course, it was about a pregnancy.

"I have literally never talked about my uterus this much. Ever." She leaned forward with an almost feral smile on her face. "Are we going to talk about your dicks next or just my internal organs? Should we start with length? Girth? STI screenings?"

She was happy to take the baby talk from Irma, but not Santos's brothers. Not today. Not any day.

Juan and Francisco's faces reddened with shame as they shook their heads.

"Didn't think so," Mary said smugly.

"Sorry," they mumbled in unison.

"I accept your apology," she cried happily. "And I'm not pregnant. We just want to give you guys your presents all at once."

"Is it an iPad?"

"Definitely not."

They sighed in disappointment before turning back to their phones.

Irma's laughter filtered down the hall before she and Knox stepped into the living room. She waved at Mary at the same time the front door opened and Santos walked inside with his father.

"Okay, muchachos," Irma said. "What is this all about? I have menudo to make."

Santos's face was red from the frigid winter air and he was fidgeting with the envelope in his hands. She frowned as he started crushing the bow she'd affixed to the front in his nervous grasp. He shook his head and rushed to Mary's side, shoving the envelope into her hands. They'd decided that Santos should give his family their present; apparently, he'd changed his mind. She grabbed the gift from his hand and straightened the crushed bow. When she looked up, everyone's eyes were trained on her, a little *too* excited for her liking.

"So first of all, I am *not* pregnant."

Irma sighed sadly before nodding. "Next Christmas. After the wedding," she replied confidently, as if she was speaking it into existence. Mary's mouth fell open in shock and Knox faked a small coughing fit to hide his laughter. Santos was quiet as a mouse.

Mary took a deep, calming breath before she yanked the conversation back on track. "We, um... We weren't sure what to get you all for Christmas," she said, turning to look each member of the Santos family briefly in the eye.

"Tablets," Francisco coughed into his hand.

"Still no," Mary smiled, much to his disappointment. "After giving it some serious consideration, we thought that maybe you guys would like to come visit us."

"In Sea Breeze?" Juan said.

"Sea Port," Knox and Santos corrected.

"Which is where?" Francisco asked.

"So far away," Irma cut in. "But we can decorate the nursery." She sounded more excited as she spoke and walked across the living room, pulling Mary into a tight, excited hug.

Knox covered his mouth with his fist while Mary glared at him over Irma's shoulder.

"Or you can just visit us, mamí. You can take a vacation," Santos offered.

"Are there clubs there?" Juan asked.

Knox actually laughed louder.

This was getting completely out of hand, but Irma gave great hugs, so Mary gave in. Just a little bit. "I like yellow," she mumbled into Irma's shoulder.

"That's a good neutral color," José added helpfully.

"Wait, do we all have to come together?" Francisco asked when Irma finally released Mary from her arms.

"No. You can use the tickets whenever you want."

"Cool. We'll come down before you get pregnant," Juan announced.

"And we'll come down after," Irma said confidently as she moved to pull her son into a hug. "Unless you decide to move closer?"

"Mamá," Santos sighed in an exasperated tone.

"We won't be doing that," Mary sighed. "But you'll always be welcome."

"Absolutely," Knox laughed.

"We'll talk," Irma whispered as she moved around Mary to hug Knox next.

Mary handed the envelope with the paperwork over to José and he accepted it with an adorable fatherly wink.

"Will you bring tamales?" Knox asked.

"Tamales for babies," Irma said.

"Deal," Knox replied happily.

Santos rolled his eyes and shook his head. Mary smiled sheepishly at him. "Shoulda stuck to the plan," she hissed.

"So...are there clubs in Sea Board or not?" Juan asked again.

HAPPY HOLIDAYS FROM SEA PORT

Mary

The Santos household was at capacity. It had to be. There were people in every room, in every chair, even outside — front and back. Everywhere she turned, Mary ran into a member of the Santos family, but not Santos. She'd been searching for him all over the house, most recently in the backyard because Juan said he saw Miguel out there. Maybe he had been at one point, but not now. She needed to find Santos so he could find Knox because she hadn't seen either man in an hour.

She turned back toward the house and stepped aside as one of Santos's uncles pushed through the door. He held the door open for her with a smile on his face. "Gracias," she mumbled under her breath, embarrassment heating her face at her stumbling pronunciation.

She walked from the back door through the hallway and yelped when an arm wrapped around her waist, yanking her into a small room off the back door. Thankfully, she recognized the arm, the chest, and the cologne. Mary relaxed into Knox's hold while he pushed a red Solo cup into her hand.

"Don't panic, but I'm drunk as hell," Knox slurred. "Hide this."

"What's happening? Where have you been?"

"Hey, Mary," a small voice said. "Oh...hey, Knox."

He cleared his throat and stepped directly behind Mary. "Hey, Beatriz," he called, a soft slur in his words.

Santos's cousin Beatriz was looking straight through Mary, eyes trained on Knox and practically twinkling. Mary knew teenage infatuation when she saw it.

"Beatriz, have you seen Sa— Miguel? Our Miguel?" she clarified.

"Nope. You okay, Knox?" Beatriz asked, leaning around her to get a clearer view of Knox.

"No. Absolutely not," Knox said, holding onto Mary's waist like a lifeline. "Goddamn Hector won't leave me or my hot chocolate alone. It's more rum than chocolate at this point. I need food."

Mary felt for him, but she couldn't help but giggle a little at his distress. They'd been worried how Santos's extended family would treat them, but as usual, everyone loved Knox the moment they met him, and Santos's uncle showed that love through *very* strong drinks. It was funny and ridiculous all at the same time.

Thankfully, Beatriz had her head on straight. "Go to the kitchen," she said, leaning around Mary. "Every woman in that kitchen will feed you without being asked."

Knox's face relaxed in relief. "Thanks for the tip, kid." He squeezed Mary's waist and immediately walked away.

Beatriz frowned as Knox darted into the kitchen, but

then teenage delusion lifted her mood. "He's so hot," she sighed.

"He's okay," Santos teased, appearing at the back door. She'd been looking for both men for so long and then they just appeared — and in Knox's case, disappeared — in minutes.

Santos walked around Beatriz to stand next to Mary. He threw his arm around her shoulders and she leaned into his side.

Beatriz was unimpressed with Santos's assessment. "You're just jealous of him."

Mary covered her mouth with her palm and let herself laugh.

"Jealous of Knox? Why would I be jealous of him?"

"Because he's hot," she said. "And you're..." She let her voice trail off and gave her cousin an appraising gaze. Clearly, she found him lacking in the looks department when compared to Knox. "And he has the best smile," Beatriz added, really sticking the knife in deeper.

"She does have a point," Mary laughed, which granted her a few seconds of Beatriz's approval.

Santos grunted his agreement before speaking. "Your mom's looking for you."

Those words froze the triumphant smile on Beatriz's face. "Why?"

He shrugged. "Not sure. She had a roll of trash bags in her hand, though."

Her eyes widened and she darted around them toward the stairs. "Bye, Mary!" she yelled over her shoulder, fleeing for her life. They just barely heard her hurried footsteps over the music blaring from a dated but still effective home stereo system they'd set up in the dining room.

"Is her mother really looking for her?" she asked.

Santos shrugged again. "She will be eventually. Come dance with me."

"Absolutely not," Mary gasped. "Wait. You dance?"

Santos's mouth lifted into the biggest smile Mary had ever seen on his face.

"Are you drunk?" she asked.

"Very. Pinche Hector."

"And you want to dance?"

For most of the day she'd stood on the sidelines, watching as Santos's aunts, uncles, and cousins of all ages had flowed on and off the dance floor they'd constructed from a slab of hardwood in the middle of the emptied formal dining room. When his cousins started looking in her direction, Mary had dipped out of there real quick, but Santos's drunken smile and big hands on her hips made her change her mind.

He led her down the hall and onto the dance floor. The music changed from something fast and horn-heavy that intimidated the hell out of her to something slower with lots of guitar just as they stepped into the room. The song was beautiful, but maybe a little too sexy for dancing in front of Santos's family. If he thought the same, it didn't stop him from maneuvering them into the middle of the crush of bodies. Rather than the young teenagers eager to have a good, rowdy time, the people on the dance floor now were mostly older married couples swaying slowly together.

Santos pulled her close.

He smelled like Knox. They wore the same spicy cologne

and it blended perfectly with chocolate and tequila. He smelled like home.

His mouth brushed the shell of her ear. "You having fun?"

Mary could always tell when Santos was nervous. She could hear it in the earnest shake of his voice. She could feel it in the way he held onto her, hands at the small of her back, pulling her into him as close as drunken decorum would allow. She could practically taste it on the air around him.

His words sent shivers down her spine.

"I know you were worried about coming here," he sighed. "But are you okay? Are you having fun?"

That fight was so long ago, Mary couldn't even remember it, but Santos did. She could hear it in his shaking voice.

She turned her head toward him so his lips brushed across her cheek. Their mouths were close and his eyes were wet and warm from too much tequila and emotion. She brushed her lips against his. "I was worried," she admitted, "but I was wrong. I love your family."

She felt his lips shift into a smile. "Is that the tequila talking?" he asked.

She licked his bottom lip with the tip of her tongue. "Yeah, but when that wears off, I'll feel the same."

"Are you sure?" he asked in a shaky voice.

She nodded slightly. "But if I'm wrong, you and Knox are welcome to convince me again." She kissed him softly. "With or without tequila."

His smile wasn't small now. Santos, the serious, snarky, messy man she loved, led her in a slow circle in the middle of the dance floor, smiling at her for his entire family to see.

The only thing that could have made this better was if Knox was here, but the night was young.

This was only the beginning of the trip. Mary couldn't know what lay ahead of them — who might greet them with open arms and who'd turn them away — but in that moment, she didn't care. Those slow minutes on the dance floor with Santos, surrounded by his family, knowing that his mother and aunts were in the kitchen heaping mountains of food onto Knox's plate, obliterated the fear that had dogged her since they left their little cul-de-sac.

They'd built a strong foundation in Sea Port and now Mary knew nothing on this trip could shake it.

I t was their last night in Denver and Mary had been fighting tears all day; even Santos wasn't this weepy. She wanted to sob into another plate of leftover cochinita pibil, but there was baking to be done and Mary wouldn't miss it.

The entire house woke up hungover. Mary dragged herself up to the main floor where Irma was already in the kitchen brewing coffee, ready for a full day of baking.

"Let them rise for at least forty minutes," Irma instructed, gesturing toward the formed balls of dough on the butcher block counter.

Mary nodded, tapping away at the notes she'd been taking on her tablet. She was trying to keep her notes organized but her brain was sluggish at best. When they went over the recipe, it had seemed pretty straightforward, but once they got started, things had gone left. Apparently, Irma's recipes were bases on which to build rather than a prescription. She kept a keen eye on the dough, adjusting measurements for a feel she couldn't describe. She didn't use electric mixers and even hungover, every dough was perfect. By noon, Mary was in awe of Irma and fighting back memories of being in the kitchen with her grandfather.

Mary became Irma's apprentice. She never went to culinary school, but one day in Irma Santos's kitchen felt like a crash course that scratched that itch. When she made it back to Sea Port, top of Mary's list would be to remind Bria how good she had it in Confections.

They were waiting for the formed conchas to rise one more time while the men watched football in the living room. They'd stuck their heads into the kitchen every now and then, sometimes pretending to say hello, sometimes squeezing through to get fresh beers, but always with their eyes on the concha production line. Santos was the worst, though, his eyes wide as he waited for each new batch of treats. He kept a close eye on the oven as if it was calling his name.

He dumped the empty beer cans into the recycling bin and walked to the fridge for more, his eyes trained on the tray of rising pastries.

"Go away, Miguelito," Irma teased. She was bent over a large stockpot of steaming tamales. This special batch was going into the deep freezer overnight for Knox. Well, technically, it was for all of them, but Irma was making them for Knox.

The conchas were for Miguel.

"I'm going," Santos said, walking slowly from the room.

His eyes never left the dough, not even as he kissed his mother on the cheek.

"Gordito," she whispered affectionately as he disappeared back into the living room.

Mary liked seeing Santos so at home. He was still the tall, silent man whose favorite pastimes were getting Knox hard and making her wet, but now he was also a walking sweet tooth who adored his mother. This trip had unlocked a brand-new dimension of the Santos she loved.

"Okay, Mary," Irma said seemingly out of the blue. "Now we bake the conchas until they're **golden brown**." She stressed those last two words, so Mary bolded them in the recipe before setting her tablet aside to help Irma load them into the oven.

"And now we wait," Irma said.

"And clean," Mary added, already rolling her sleeves up to tackle the full sink.

Irma shook her head and clucked her tongue. "That's for the men," she said and then called Paco to get started. "Remember that," she said.

"Yes, ma'am!" Mary beamed.

Instead of watching the conchas bake, she went to the living room to check on the other men. Juan was sitting on the floor in front of the largest couch, typing away on his phone. José was sitting in a recliner, pretending to watch the game while he dozed off. Her men were sitting side-by-side on the smaller couch, Santos's arm thrown over Knox's shoulders. Mary was overcome with the urge to cry all over again.

Maybe he felt her gaze on them or maybe he was more focused on the kitchen than the game; either way, Mary wasn't surprised when Santos turned toward the door. He raised his eyebrows in excitement and Mary shook her head, raising one finger on her right hand while opening her left. Fifteen minutes until he could have a concha, she told him silently.

He smiled and pulled Knox closer, turning back to a game Mary was sure no one besides José was watching.

She walked back into the kitchen and picked up her tablet, writing a note in the margins of this recipe.

ULTIMATE BRIBE: SANTOS

By the time the conchas were ready, Knox and Santos had already moved to the kitchen, setting up a casual vigil at the table, almost certainly at Santos's urging. Irma put a couple of conchas on a plate in front of them. Santos immediately snatched one soft ball up and pulled it apart, steam erupting into the air. In the moment just before he took his first bite, Santos looked like a happy child. Irma smiled down at her eldest son with glassy eyes.

Knox leaned into Mary's side. "I ain't ever seen him smile this much." Mary nodded in quick agreement.

Irma lovingly rubbed a hand through Santos's hair. "Eat. Enjoy," she said to Mary and Knox before grabbing another platter of conchas and walking into the living room.

When it was just the three of them, Knox and Mary watched Santos eat half a concha in silence. He looked innocently happy and, without his mother's presence, a little sexy. He was in pure ecstasy and they didn't want to interrupt his joy.

Their silence was broken by Paco's excited cry announcing a touchdown.

"I'm happy we came," Mary whispered, breaking open her own sweet bread.

Knox nodded, licking sugar from his fingers. Santos smiled, but he was eyeing the platter of cooling pastries on the kitchen counter, so Mary wasn't sure at first if he'd really heard her.

"How happy?" Santos asked, eyeing her with a sexy grin.

It was shocking how quickly two words could change the mood between them. One second Santos looked ready to shove a concha in his mouth whole, the next he looked hungry for something else.

Knox pressed his thigh against hers under the table. She eyed Santos before leaning into Knox's side and whispering into his ear. She made sure her voice carried to Santos. "Irma gave me the recipe for the conchas and her orejas as well."

Santos groaned loudly.

Knox turned to her with eyebrows bunched in confusion. "What's that?"

"Did I say that right?" Mary asked, looking to Santos for confirmation.

"I'm going to fuck you two into next week," he groaned, standing from the table to snatch another concha from the counter. Mary and Knox's eyes went straight to the prominent bulge in his pants.

"Who cares what they are? Make him a dozen."

SANTOS

S antos didn't cry often. He couldn't even remember the last thing that had brought him to tears. He wasn't emotionally repressed, he just wasn't the kind of person who resorted to tears unless there was a damn good reason. Hugging his parents and brothers goodbye in the pre-dawn cold was a damn good reason.

Five days hadn't been long enough, but it was a start. They'd said this kind of goodbye dozens of times before, but this one seemed harder and easier somehow. He held himself together through each hug — even the surprisingly tight ones from his little brothers — but when his dad got too choked up to speak, he almost broke down on their front porch. His mother was just about to ask them to stay when she stopped herself. He couldn't have said yes and he appreciated that she respected Knox and Mary enough not to put him in the position to tell her no. They hugged the longest.

Santos held himself together until they were on the freeway heading west and then tears fell from his eyes like small rivers.

Knox was at the wheel and rested his hand on Santos's knee. Mary wrapped her arms around the seat and his chest, her fingers tickling his beard. They stayed that way for nearly twenty miles, silently holding him through the hardest goodbye he'd had since he was eighteen and his family saw him off to boot camp.

It was miles before he felt ready to speak again. He might have held out longer, but Knox found an '80s pop radio station and he and Mary started singing loudly and amazingly off-key.

Santos shut the radio off. "That's enough of that," he mumbled into the shocking quiet.

"You could've just asked us to keep it down."

"And you would have kept singing," he said, kissing her hand.

Knox burst out laughing and tossed his phone into Santos's lap so he could find something else for them to listen to.

If someone had told Santos two months ago that they'd be driving to Vegas with frozen tamales in a cooler in the trunk and a bag full of conchas Mary made with his mother in the back seat, he wouldn't have believed it, but it was happening. They were living it.

Knox and Mary were part of his family and they were building a family of their own. This was the life he'd been praying for.

HAPPY HOLIDAYS FROM SEA PORT

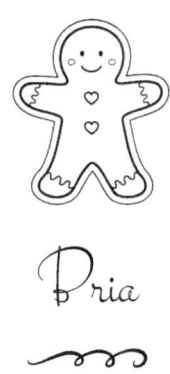

Bria

"Cinnamon rolls or breakfast sandwiches?" Bria asked.

It was hours to sunrise but Bria was lounging in Sully's bed, naked and happy.

Sully kissed a path down Bria's spine, her fingers tickling her sides. She lifted her mouth from Bria's skin. "Confections makes breakfast sandwiches?"

Bria shivered as Sully's words raised goosebumps over her skin. "No, but that's a good idea. Never mind, we don't have the prep room to start making eggs and bacon."

That last word came out like a strangled moan because Sully had the nerve to lick halfway up her spine and retrace her steps with soft kisses while she massaged Bria's ass. There was a lot going on and all of it was delicious.

Sully pulled Bria's cheeks apart delicately. "We could do it," she whispered.

Bria spread her legs for Sully's searching fingers. "Do what?" she moaned.

Sully sucked Bria's earlobe into her mouth while one hand teased her perineum down to her opening.

"Fuck yes," Bria sighed.

"We could make the breakfast sandwiches," Sully whispered.

"Okay," Bria groaned. "What?"

Her clit jumped at Sully's laughter. "Confections could make the English muffins and we'll make the rest."

Bria clutched the pillow under her head as Sully's fingers sawed back and forth inside her. "Oh, right. Yeah," she moaned. "Okay, I'll ask Mary when she's back."

"Tell her it was your idea," Sully sighed, moving her knees to either side of Bria's hips and pressing her pussy against Bria's skin.

"Huh?" It was hardly a word, just one long, needy moan.

"It was your idea," Sully repeated.

"Right."

Sully moved her hips in time with her thrusting fingers.

"Right. Right. Fuck, there. Right." Sully wrapped her hand around the column of her throat. "Oooh fuck, that's good."

She thrust harder. Her fingers moved deeper.

Between their long hours at work, their late nights full of sex, and their early mornings full of the same, Bria and Sully were running on a little less sleep than they needed. One day, the lack of rest would catch up to them, but Bria wasn't willing to change a thing. Not when Sully's fingers were pressing against her g-spot while she rubbed her own clit on Bria's right butt cheek because what could be better than this?

Certainly not one of their phones ringing before dawn.

Bria glared at her phone lighting up like a Christmas tree, ruining the mood. Sully started to climb off her but Bria shook her head, reaching for it. "Stay there. Wait. It's probably nothing," she panted. "The fuck?"

"Why is Lorraine calling you this early?" Sully asked.

"I don't know, but if it's not life or death, it will be."

Sully laughed against Bria's shoulder.

"What, Lorraine?"

"Oop, don't be rude."

"If you don't call me before dawn, I won't have to be."

"It's not *before* dawn," Lorraine corrected.

Bria glanced at the window, saddened at the shockingly light blue sky. They were running out of time to fuck. "Even worse. Why are you calling?"

Lorraine sighed in frustration, but when she spoke, her voice was riddled with stress. "Okay, don't freak out, but I kinda fucked up."

"Um, okay. Well, you're the head librarian, so I think you'll be fine."

"Not at the library," Lorraine said. "I'm great at my job, actually."

"Okay, congrats. Bye now," Bria said. She was just about to hang up when Lorraine screamed into the phone.

"I can't find Cat-leen!" Her voice was loud enough for Sully to hear.

"Fuck," Bria ground out.

"I'll make coffee," Sully said, pulling her fingers from Bria's pussy and kissing her shoulder.

"Fuck," Bria repeated. "We'll be there in a bit."

"Oh my god, thank you!"

Bria hung up on Lorraine. It was rude and she didn't care. They were all screwed.

HAPPY HOLIDAYS FROM SEA PORT

Las Vegas

MARY

Mary loved to travel, even though she wished she'd done more of it when she was younger. One of her favorite things to do was just assume Knox and Santos had been all over the world, but their reality was more complicated than that.

Knox had been all over Europe and Asia, traveling on his downtime, desperate to see the world after a childhood narrowed to a pinpoint by his parents. One of Mary's favorite pastimes was to bake cookies while he told her oddly specific stories about cities she'd always wanted to visit. Sometimes Santos featured in the story, sometimes not. Santos normally used his leave time to go home, eat his mother's cooking, and help his dad with home repairs, or to travel to wherever Knox was stationed and pretend they were *just* friends. Mary wished he'd taken his parents on vacation or at least gagged on Knox's dick in new locations, but they couldn't go back and change the past, so they tried to soak up every ounce of this first trip together.

First but not last.

Mary spent most of their drive into Vegas spitballing all the cities and countries she wanted them to see together. Her excitement was infectious and a useful distraction from the fact that they were all getting sick of being cooped up in their car and sleeping on cheap mattresses. After a string of bad motels, Mary thought they deserved a little luxury. And by luxury, she meant a king-sized bed.

They woke up rested, happy, and hornier than usual.

Knox climbed out of bed before Mary was ready to let him go. She clung onto him until the last moment, until her nails scraped his skin.

"Ouch, fuck," he laughed, bouncing to his feet.

"Come back," she whined, hanging half off the bed, her voice thick with sleep.

"No, I gotta pee."

"Me too," she said.

"Then come on." He stopped at the foot of the bed, looking rumpled and well-rested in a sexy pair of boxers Mary would happily help him take off.

She reached for him, but Santos had her in a death grip, his arms and legs wrapped around her body. She wasn't going anywhere. Knox chuckled as he walked off to the bathroom without her.

Mary reached for the edge of the bed and tried pulling herself free of Santos's grasp. Tried and failed.

"Five more minutes," Santos grumbled in his sleep.

As soon as she relaxed, he pulled her back into his grip like a well-loved stuffed toy. Mary sighed, wiggled her ass back into his body, and stared at the bathroom door in resignation.

"Three more minutes," Santos said, shoving his face into her curls.

"Knox is up already," she whispered.

The shift was subtle, but Mary felt Santos waking up by degrees, faster than before. His hold on her loosened, his breaths came a little faster, his hips ground into her ass, and eventually she felt his lips pressing against her scalp.

Mary scratched the arm he'd wrapped around her like a seatbelt. "I think we can all fit in the shower."

They didn't move for a second. Santos didn't even breathe until Knox flushed the toilet and the sink turned on. Mary listened to Knox wash his hands, waiting patiently for Santos to come fully awake. Knox started whistling and Santos finally released her.

Mary sat up eagerly and smoothed her hands over Santos's chest as he rubbed sleep from his eyes.

Knox walked back into the room, still whistling, still smiling.

Santos finally sat up in bed. "Get naked," he said in a voice still thick with sleep.

"Um, me or him?" Mary asked, happy as a clam.

Santos glared over his shoulder. "Both. Obviously."

"Yeah, obviously," Knox echoed, laughing his ass off, already pulling his tank top up his chest.

"Shower," she said in a deep voice, trying to imitate Santos, but succeeding in making Knox laugh just a bit harder. She pushed at Santos's back until he stood from the bed. Santos helped her to stand while they both watched Knox, his fingers toying with the waistband of his boxers.

"See what a good night's sleep will do?" she whispered,

skipping toward the bathroom as soon as her feet hit the carpet.

"We will," Santos yawned.

They'd been careful in Santos's parents' basement. Sure, they'd fucked like bunnies damn near every night and a few mornings, but they'd done so respectfully, quietly. The bed frame squeaked, so they had slow sex and kept Mary's mouth full enough to muffle her screams. That was a lot of fun. But for the next few days, Mary was looking forward to letting loose.

Knox turned on the shower while Mary undressed. Santos wrapped his arms around her body and cradled her heavy breasts in his big hands, rolling her nipples between his fingers while Knox watched.

Knox finally pushed his boxers down his legs and watched Santos play with Mary for a few moments while his dick slowly inflated. After a while, he shoved his hand in the shower stall. "Almost hot enough," he sighed and grabbed his erection with his wet hand.

Mary reached between her legs to massage her clit. "Feels pretty hot to me," she moaned.

Knox walked toward them dick-first with a hungry smile on his face. "You might have a point."

She felt Santos's smile against her pulse. The walk-in shower was plenty big enough for all of them.

SANTOS

He needed a strong cup of coffee to wake his brain up for the day. Or an orgasm that made his toes curl; whatever got the neurons firing. Today, he watched Mary push Knox against the shower wall, laughing as she kissed his pulse and stroked his dick. Knox hadn't come yet and Mary was decidedly unhappy about that. Santos was taking a break to wash his hair just in case the hot water gave out, lathering the shampoo in his hair and enjoying the show.

Knox caressed Mary's soft back, but his gaze was firmly set on Santos. She kissed a path to his ear and started whispering to him. Santos would ask about whatever filthy things she was saying later, but right now, he just wanted to enjoy that whatever she was saying made Knox happy. She stroked Knox's shaft slowly, rotating her hand, squeezing the head, tickling his balls. Santos got careless with the suds and flinched when shampoo slipped into his eyes, so he backed under the shower spray and rinsed the soap from his hair.

When he could see clearly again, Mary had turned to face him, massaging her breasts while Knox took his turn to whisper in her ear as they both watched him.

Santos reached for his own shaft and stroked himself just as a filthy moan fell from Mary's lips.

"Where are your hands, Sergeant?" Santos asked in a rough voice.

Mary's eyes were hooded with desire, her bottom lip wet from her tongue. The ends of her hair stuck to her face and neck. She sucked in a strangled cry when Knox moved her feet apart with one of his own, giving Santos a clear view of his hand between her thighs.

Santos took a step forward, but Mary shook her head and gasped out one word. "Conditioner."

"Really?"

"You're not gonna be pissed at me just 'cause you're too horny to finish washing your hair. Besides, I love how soft your hair is." She let out a cute giggle that was also a filthy moan. "Knox said he likes it too."

"Can Knox speak?" Santos asked, glaring at the man whose mouth was glued to Mary's ear, his tongue tasting her earlobe.

Mary's head listed forward and her eyes closed in ecstasy. "He said condition your hair and you can find out." Her hips circled over his fingers.

Santos did as he was told.

Knox and Mary got wilder.

While Santos was raking the conditioner through his hair, Knox bent Mary forward. He removed his fingers from between her legs, held her at the waist, and eased inside her. Mary's next moan was long, deep, and it felt like electricity crackling down his spine. She reached back to grab Knox's wrists for leverage as he moved her body forward and back along his length. Mary closed her eyes and let Knox use her while he stared Santos down, the promise that he would fuck Santos just like this when it was his turn. Santos and Knox locked eyes as Mary moaned louder and louder between them. There were few things that made Santos so hard his dick hurt; watching Knox and Mary fuck was one of them, and they knew it.

"Oh my god! Fuck," Mary screamed, toes curling and legs shaking. The only thing holding her upright was Knox's firm grip, and he gathered her against his chest and fucked her through another orgasm that had tears leaking from her eyes.

Knox whispered to Mary again, giving Santos a dirty, smug smile just before he stepped under the spray to clean his hair. That smile asked Santos if he wanted some of what he gave Mary, and the answer was yes. Always yes.

Santos turned the water spigot off just as Mary lifted off of Knox's dick. She disentangled herself from his arms with a bemused look on her face, taking a second to calm her shaking legs. Santos reached out to catch her, but she brushed past him. "He still hasn't come yet," she announced happily and stepped from the shower.

Knox was still leaning against the shower wall. Legs spread. Dick still hard and wet from Mary's pussy. Waiting.

Santos could have played coy, but he didn't want to. "You like my soft hair?"

"I do."

Santos used Knox's body for leverage as he lowered to his knees.

"That's gonna hurt like a bitch," Knox laughed.

"Not if you come quick."

Knox slipped his thick fingers into Santos's hair. "This should be fun," he whispered as Santos licked up his shaft.

This wasn't the trip he'd had in mind; it was better.

The life he lived with Knox and Mary was one he'd been too scared to believe could be real; too scared to hope that he deserved all this. He wasn't normally a crier, but in that moment — with Knox hard and wet in his mouth and Mary sighing contentedly behind them as she did her skincare — Santos felt like he was floating because he had them.

HAPPY HOLIDAYS FROM SEA PORT

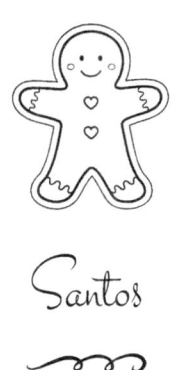

Santos

"Too bright," Santos groaned when the car stopped moving, nudging him awake. As soon as he opened his eyes, he closed them again and pulled his sunglasses onto his face. "So fucking bright."

Knox's laughter filtered in from the front seat. "Suck it up, buttercup."

"I already did that," Santos groaned again, smiling to himself at Knox's laughter.

"That you did. We're here."

When Santos's eyes adjusted to the bright desert sun, he got a clear view of a mostly empty parking lot. Knox had taken up the task of driving because he knew the way still and the other two were worn out after their joint shower. Santos dozed for most of the ride and Mary was still asleep, her head in Santos's lap. Their destination was over an hour from their hotel and the drive flew by.

Santos yawned and tried to stretch his back but Mary grumbled in her sleep. He'd stretch later.

"Where the hell'd you get that?" Santos asked as Knox took a sip from a coffee cup.

"Stopped by a coffee shop when I got off the freeway."

"How are you not tired?" Santos croaked.

"I learned to stop needing much sleep in boot camp." Knox shrugged.

"That was a million years ago. And we didn't used to spend half the night balls-deep inside each other then."

Knox chuckled softly, nearly spitting out his coffee. "Maybe we shoulda."

"Did you get me any coffee?" Santos asked, licking his lips.

"Nope."

"Gimme," he said, reaching forward. Knox chuckled some more but passed the cup into the back seat.

Santos's lips covered the spot where Knox's had just been. He closed his eyes and took a long sip of black coffee, the dark, comforting drink making him feel better from the first sip. "This it?" he asked, looking out at the empty parking lot again.

"This is it. They're not open yet, though. I tried to go the exact speed limit so y'all could get a little more sleep, but the traffic was light and here we are."

Santos absently smoothed his free hand over one of the thick cornrows on either side of Mary's head. "You excited?"

"Yeah." Knox reached back for the cup. Their fingers brushed together during the exchange. "You nervous?" he asked after another sip. Knox turned in the driver's seat now. Santos licked his lips. Knox watched him with a hooded gaze while he sucked his own bottom lip into his mouth.

"A little," Santos finally replied as their gazes met. "We've been friends for twenty years and I'm just now meeting Ms. Pearl." He didn't say it as an accusation because it wasn't one. Santos kept his voice mild even though his stomach was churning with some mixture of guilt, regret, and excitement.

"Don't do that," Knox breathed.

Santos pushed his sunglasses back onto his head. "Don't do what?"

Knox stared at him in silence for a few seconds before his mouth lifted into a smile that was all lips and just the smallest flash of teeth. Santos had seen this smile on Knox before and it always managed to make his blood pressure rise. "Don't go back and wonder what if. Our relationship played out just the way it shoulda."

Santos knew he was right, but his heart couldn't help but wonder. He'd thought about it over the years — far more times than he'd probably ever admit — and being happy in a relationship with Knox only seemed to make it worse. "But what if..." he offered with a sad smile. "What if we *had* gotten together when we first met?"

Knox laughed deep but hollow. "Considering who we were back then, we woulda fucked for a few months before one of us got bored." Santos started to object, but Knox kept going. "*Or* until one of us got stationed somewhere else. And that woulda been it."

"That's not true," Santos said, shaking his head.

"Yeah, it is. I know who I was back then and I remember who you were," he offered gently. No judgment, just understanding — the exact reason Santos had gravitated to Knox all those years ago. Knox leaned over the center console into the back seat. "Neither of us was interested in anything more serious than a steady fuck back then. We woulda fucked, it woulda been good, and it would've been over before we knew it. If we'd gotten together back then, we would've ruined our friendship 'cause we weren't ready."

Sometimes when Knox spoke, Santos felt like that eighteen-year-old recruit hanging onto his every word. What Santos hated most was that he made perfect sense. Santos had sucked and fucked his way through both his branches of service, but none of those people had been Knox. No one had ever made him feel quite like Knox did.

He leaned forward as much as possible without disturbing Mary's sleep. "It would have been different with you."

Knox laughed and extended his arm to cup Santos's cheek.

"I believe you. For what it's worth, I think it woulda been different with you too, but different don't mean it would've lasted. Right person. Wrong time," he said. His gaze dipped to Mary's sleeping face for a second. "Right persons. Right time," he added, brushing his thumb over Santos's lips.

Santos's throat was littered with things he wanted to say, things he wished he'd said years ago, but this wasn't the time or the place. Besides, most of what he wanted to say would hit harder when he could whisper them against Knox's bare skin. So for now, he kissed Knox's palm. The air in their car changed. Electricity licked up Santos's spine. Their gazes locked as Santos sucked Knox's thumb into his mouth.

He grunted softly, pressing the pad of his finger against Santos's tongue, reminding them both of the weight of Knox's dick in the same place. Of how good it had felt when he came right there just a few hours ago.

Santos's hands moved on their own, settling on Mary's face, caressing her temple while he worked over Knox's finger.

"I don't remember you loving sucking dick this much back then," Knox laughed.

Santos smiled and released Knox's finger from his mouth. "Like I said, it's different with you."

"Here, here," Mary croaked. She rolled onto her back and stretched her arms across the back seat. "Don't stop on my account," she said. "Pretend I'm not even here. Or naked."

Knox laughed, shaking his head as he lifted the coffee cup to his mouth, or tried to, at least. Mary snatched the cup from his hands and drank deeply. "Ugh. No sugar? No cream?" she groaned before taking another sip.

Santos and Knox smiled indulgently as Mary drank the last of Knox's coffee.

"Feel better?" Knox asked.

"I feel great. So, are we here, or did you pull over for a little Lorraine and Jonah time?"

Knox laughed some more while Santos rubbed soothing circles over Mary's back. "We're here. Just waiting for them to open."

"Are you nervous?" Mary asked, leaning forward to caress the back of his head.

"I was," he admitted. "I still am a little. I've never brought anyone here before. Not like this." He turned to look through the front windshield while he spoke, smiling even as his brows knit together anxiously. "We don't—"

"Don't do that," Santos said before Knox could finish the sentence. "We're not going anywhere."

"I was just—"

Mary sucked her teeth in annoyance. "You were just gonna tell us we don't have to stay, or we can stay in the car if we want." She lowered her voice, trying to mimic Knox's deep tone.

"I don't sound like that," he sighed.

"Yeah, you do."

He glanced at Santos for help but found none.

"Yeah, you do. Anyway, you're always working double time to put everyone else at ease. Why don't you let us do that for you sometimes?"

"I do," Knox said.

"Not enough," Mary replied, echoing Santos's thoughts.

"We're here to meet your people. We've been waiting for this almost as much as you."

For a second, Knox tried to fight a beautiful smile, but that was like the earth trying to spin in the other direction. When it finally broke through, something fearful in Santos's chest settled.

"Y'all really know how to make a man feel loved," Knox whispered.

"You make it easy," Santos said in a deep, serious tone of voice.

"Very," Mary agreed. "Even if your taste in coffee sucks."

HAPPY HOLIDAYS FROM SEA PORT

Knox

K nox didn't dwell on the past, especially not his. There was all too little about his youth worthy of remembering. Some days, he felt like everything before Santos, Mary, and Sea Port was static he should tune out. Except before them, there'd been Pearl's House, the longest running soup kitchen and community center for queer people of color in Nevada.

Pearl's House opened its doors in the winter of 1981, but Ms. Pearl had been providing the same services to the community since the early Seventies. He'd heard stories from everybody but her about the tiny apartment — Pearl's actual house — on the Westside where anyone could find a safe place to sleep, a hot meal, and a change of clothes; whatever they needed. She fed people out of her own pocket until the need was too great, and then many of those same people — people who were still alive by the grace of God and Pearl — scrounged up enough money to keep her going for one more week, then one more month, until eventually, she was renting a space in a half-abandoned strip mall.

Pearl considered all the people who came through her doors as family, even if their paths only crossed once. Ms. Pearl had boundless patience for people and a unique ability to make them feel welcome and loved.

Knox met her purely by chance.

He'd been fresh out of boot camp in San Diego. Some of the other recruits wanted to celebrate with a long weekend of debauchery in Vegas. Knox was eighteen and still testing the boundaries of his newfound freedom. He didn't care where they went as long as it wasn't Texas, but he realized his mistake almost immediately.

Home was chaos — loud voices, slamming doors, breaking glass, screaming. The first night he spent away from home — in a Greyhound bus station — the quiet had been a godsend. Other recruits struggled to adjust to boot camp, but Knox had been waiting his whole life for stability. His days were regimented, his meals were hot, and after lights out, Knox drifted immediately asleep — safe for the first time in his life.

Vegas was not that. The Strip was neon bright, loud, busy, and Knox hated it almost immediately. The first day of the trip had been hell, surrounded by a pack of drunk, horny Marines acting like the Code of Conduct didn't apply off-base. He'd been seriously considering hitchhiking back to California while the other men guzzled cheap beer and catcalled girls like rabid animals set loose. That wasn't the kind of man he wanted to be.

And then he met Ms. Pearl.

They'd been lingering at a corner trying to get directions

to a strip club where Knox spotted an older Black woman across the street. She was in her late forties, in thick-soled shoes, standing on a busy corner offering little baggies to passersby. His buddies had been pooling their money for more cheap vodka as Knox watched two foot cops approach the woman, offering her a cup of coffee. Knox had stopped paying attention to his friends by then; curiosity got the best of him even if he didn't know why.

He remembered his friends calling after him, but he didn't stop. He'd dropped his beer in the closest trash can and jogged across the street, approaching her just as the cops moved along.

And as she did with everyone, Ms. Pearl had welcomed him with a warm smile.

"Hello there," Ms. Pearl had said.

"Hi," Knox breathed, smiling shyly.

"Ooh, now that smile is a killer. I just know you're popular with the girls. Maybe the boys too."

Knox's cheeks had warmed with embarrassment. He was still struggling to cope with compliments. "What'chu got there?"

She reached into the backpack hanging off one shoulder and pulled out a small plastic bag, offering it to him. "Just a little care package," she'd said.

He grasped the bag and inspected the items — condoms, a small packet of lube, wet wipes, travel toothbrush, and a small tube of toothpaste. When he tried to hand it back, she shook her head. "No, you keep that. If you don't need it, maybe someone you know will. Where's that accent from, young man?"

"Texas. A little town just outside of Austin. I'm here with my buddies," he said, gesturing across the street. He glanced

over his shoulder to find them yelling after a group of women running away. Knox shook his head and sighed.

"Army?" she asked, pulling his attention back.

"Marines," he corrected.

"You all stationed in San Diego?"

"Just made it through boot camp."

Her smile had brightened. "Congratulations. What's next?"

Knox's friends went to a strip club and he helped Ms. Pearl hand out more care packages. Most of the people he met that night had a lost look in their eyes and reminded Knox of the boy he used to be. Every baggie he gave out selfishly soothed some small part of him, so he went back the next night. Instead of handing out more care packages, Ms. Pearl drove Knox around town to collect food donations for her soup kitchen. At the end of the trip, he met the other guys at the Greyhound station tired, happy and feeling like he was starting to find himself.

Knox couldn't imagine who he'd be if he hadn't met Ms. Pearl. For the next few years, he spent every holiday and most of his regular leave in Vegas, helping Ms. Pearl and her son, Marcus, serve the local community. He sent her money from his wages and postcards from around the world, always surprised when he received a letter in return. When people asked about home, he talked about Ms. Pearl, Marcus, and all the volunteers he'd met at Pearl's House. It took years, but Ms. Pearl gave Knox the kind of safety he'd dreamed about as a child, and all she asked was that he pay some of that forward whenever he could.

They crawled from the car and stretched, muscles still aching from all of the time spent on the road trip and early morning sex. Mary slipped her hand into Knox's as they joined the slow trickle of people lining up outside Pearl's House.

The first time Knox came here, the strip mall had felt desolate, but there'd still been a few businesses hanging on. All these years later, Pearl's House seemed to be one of the last establishments left. Eventually, some developer would buy this land and probably turn it into another strip mall and then sell it again before it became a hotel. But Pearl's House would be here until the end, holding space for the people society wanted to throw away.

Pearl's House had one big picture window and the team had decorated it with fake snow and Christmas-themed decals. It was festive, but it had nothing on the Santos decorations. They stepped into line behind a group of teenagers, excitedly chatting at one another like parrots first thing in the morning. Knox had seen so many kids like this over the years, but for the first time, seeing those kids didn't make him sorrowful about his childhood; he was just happy they had somewhere to go.

Santos was being...Santos, standing at Knox and Mary's back, head swiveling right to left taking in the crowd and the parking lot around them, looking like an armed bodyguard.

And Mary was being Mary. "I love your eye makeup," she told one of the kids in front of them. Their eyelids were covered in a thick black swoop that wasn't to Knox's liking, but Mary was smiling so earnestly. The group turned around en masse and gave Mary a critical once-over Knox didn't enjoy. And neither did Santos because he stepped closer at her back, pulling their attention to him.

"You look like a cop," said a girl in Dickies and a button-up flannel shirt with even heavier black eyeliner and a deep purple matte lipstick.

"He is," Mary replied cheerily, but her smile faltered when they took a step back. "Oh, don't worry. He's not a cop here."

"A cop is a cop," one of the other kids said.

"True," Mary said gently. "I'm sorry. We'll leave you alone. But seriously, really great eye shadow," she said, smiling at them with the same warmth as before, except this time it worked and they seemed appropriately dazzled by her. Knox and Santos approved of that response, not that the kids cared.

"Thanks," they eventually replied in unison before turning around and getting back to their conversation.

"Billy? Billy, is that you?"

Knox would recognize that voice anywhere and stepped out of line to find a familiar figure walking in his direction.

"Oh shit, look at you!" Marcus yelled happily.

They slapped hands and Knox let Marcus pull him into a hug. "What's up, Marcus? Long time, no see."

When they pulled back from one another, Knox looked his old friend over with a smile, and besides the small smattering of salt in his facial hair, he looked just about the same as Knox remembered.

"Pearl said you might be stopping through."

"She here?"

"Yeah, yeah, she's in the kitchen. Come on."

"These two are with me," Knox said, gesturing toward Mary and Santos.

Santos put a hand at Mary's back as Marcus's gaze

shifted in their direction. "Hi," Mary called cheerily. Santos nodded once in greeting.

"Mmmhmm," Marcus said, smiling back. "Well, come on, then. There's work to do."

Knox made sure Mary and Santos were behind him as he followed his old friend inside.

"What work?" Mary whispered.

They squeezed past the crowd through the front door into a building that looked about the same as Knox remembered. The line outside led straight into an equally long line for food and opened up to a large dining room beyond that. Knox had never known this room to be empty unless they were closed. The crowd always managed to warm his heart and devastate him at the same time.

They followed Marcus down a short hallway that led to a crowded, hot kitchen. This room, too, looked about the same as Knox remembered — maybe a newish appliance or two — and then he caught his first glimpse of Ms. Pearl in nearly three years, standing on a stool in front of the second-hand commercial stove they'd bought a few years ago. She was stirring a ladle in a pot half as tall as her while yelling directions at the rest of the staff. That's when he knew he was home.

"Mama!" Marcus called. "Mama, look who's here."

She turned halfway around and her entire dark, wrinkled face lit up when her eyes landed on Knox. "Billy!"

Knox was across the kitchen before she even finished saying his name. His throat was dry as all the moisture in his body moved to his tear ducts.

"Oooh, boy, look at you. You're getting old," she said, rubbing his back as he hugged her tight.

"You're one to talk," Knox laughed.

"It's a gift," she said softly, patting his back. "Remember that. Every wrinkle and gray hair is a gift."

He squeezed one more time before releasing her, his arm still around her shoulders. "You hear that, Marcus? Every gray hair is a gift."

The other man rolled his eyes. "You barely been here a minute and already getting on my nerves."

"That's how you know it's real," she laughed. "Oh, now who's this you brought with you?"

Knox helped Ms. Pearl down from her stool and led her across the room to introduce her to Mary and Santos.

"It's so good to meet you, Ms. Pearl," Mary said. "Knox has told us so much about you."

"He loves you a lot."

She squinted at them for long, silent seconds, until even Mary's smile started to falter, before turning to Knox. "Is this the Santos from the Marines?"

"Yes, ma'am, it is."

The smile on her face matched Mary's as she moved toward Santos, reaching for his hands. He looked surprised and confused, his face reddening as she approached.

"I've been waiting a long while to meet you," she said simply.

Santos's eyes flitted to Knox. "I've been waiting a while to meet you too, Ms. Pearl."

She patted his hands before turning in Mary's direction. "And you're Mary," she said. No question necessary. "Knox told me something about you making the best biscuits he's ever tasted."

"Well…" Her voice trailed off as she tried to sound modest. "I don't know if it's the *best* biscuit."

Knox swallowed a laugh at her rookie mistake.

"I'll be the judge of that," Ms. Pearl said, all business, startling Mary. "Marcus will show you to your station."

Mary's eyes went wide and her mouth fell open. "Oh. Okay. Y-yes, ma'am." Marcus motioned for her to follow him. She looked over her shoulder, smiling warily as she disappeared to the back of the kitchen.

Ms. Pearl turned back to Santos. "I heard something about tamales."

"Oh, yes, they're in the cooler in the car."

She frowned up at him. "We can't eat them from the car now, can we?"

"Uh, no, ma'am. I'll be right back," he said. Knox tossed him their keys and laughed.

"And you—" Ms. Pearl started as Santos rushed from the room.

Knox cut her off with a resigned sigh. "I know, I know, chopping vegetables as usual."

"Mmhmm," Ms. Pearl said, giving him a pat on the back. "With that smile, the line for carrots is gonna be half a mile long."

Knox snagged an apron from the wall, washed his hands, and grabbed a knife at the vegetable station. The young person already there had pulled their long dreadlocks into a hair net and smiled gratefully when they realized Knox was there to help. They looked nothing like the eighteen-year-old Knox had been the first time he'd manned this station, but he recognized himself in the other person's eyes all the same.

HAPPY HOLIDAYS FROM SEA PORT

Santos

His mother's tamales were gone before he knew it. They were so good, the kid in the Dickies with the severe eyeliner had almost smiled when she came back for seconds. Mary's biscuits went almost as quick. Mary herself was also very popular, naturally. From his station, Santos watched her from the corner of his eye as she smiled and flirted with the never-ending line of guests, who smiled and blushed and stammered over her. Feeding people was Mary's happy place and she was almost as popular on the serving line as Knox.

Almost.

Santos assumed Ms. Pearl put Knox on vegetables because he couldn't cook, but he realized his mistake. No one had to eat everything they had on offer, but Ms. Pearl liked to give people an incentive to create a balanced plate. Knox was that incentive. If they wanted to flirt with him up close, they had to accept a spoonful of peas and carrots for the pleasure, and most people did. At some point, the line to spend just a few seconds in his presence was half as long as the line for meat. The vegetable station in the kitchen was working double time to keep his trays full.

Santos had never worked at a soup kitchen before. The amount of work was overwhelming and he couldn't help but think about all the leave Knox had spent here, working just as hard on his time off. The work was hot, sweaty, and back-breaking, but Santos had never had more fun. And every time he caught a quick glimpse of Knox in the corner of his eye, his heart ached at the young man who'd needed a place like this to survive.

At some point, Ms. Pearl pulled Knox off the service line. Santos watched her lead him around the dining room, introducing him to patrons, maybe even reintroducing him based on the big bear hugs a few of the older guests gave him. Knox moved different at Pearl's House. His shoulders slumped forward in humility, he ran his hand over the back of his neck, and Knox smiled with the kind of bashfulness that made Santos fall in love with him at eighteen.

"Hey," Mary whispered, coming up on his right side.

"What's up?"

"Out of biscuits again," she said, beaming.

"Congratulations. You making more?"

"Not me. Marcus is on it. Our shift's over."

"Oh?"

"Yeah, come on."

Santos turned back to the woman standing in front of him, waiting patiently for him to place a chicken thigh onto her plate. "Okay, just one more," he said and served her with his best smile.

He was going in for another when Mary put a hand over his. "Put the tongs down and let someone else take over."

Santos was about to protest when someone with bright green eye shadow and winged liner shaped like a Christmas tree appeared behind her, clearly waiting for them to get the hell out of the way.

He sighed loudly but set the tongs to the side.

"I know, babe," Mary laughed. "I had fun too. Come on." She led him back into the kitchen where Marcus was still working.

"Y'all get washed up and get a meal," Marcus said.

"Oh, no. We're not..." Mary started.

"Everybody who works, eats," he said as if he'd had this conversation with more than a few people. "Billy's been waiting to eat with y'all."

"Alright," Santos said, a hand on Mary's shoulder. There was a small smile on Marcus's face just before they turned away.

The lunch service was over and their bellies were full. Santos was helping some of the volunteers clean the dining room while Knox helped the kitchen staff prepare for the dinner service. Mary, on the other hand, was going over her biscuit recipe with Marcus — her gift to Pearl's House. The clients had given it their stamp of approval, and Marcus and Mary were troubleshooting adjustments for large batches and instructions for the untrained bakers on staff. It was hard mental work and Mary was having the time of her life.

When the dining room was clear, Santos took a bathroom break. He was about to head into the kitchen to help Knox when he spotted Ms. Pearl sitting at a table all by herself. She was staring out at the empty parking lot, but she turned toward Santos and beckoned him forward with an elegant wave of her hand.

He walked across the dining room feeling like there were crows circling in his gut. Mary brushed the back of his hand as he passed, a small touch of encouragement — and one Ms. Pearl didn't miss, based on the small smile on her face. There was probably nothing that happened in this building that Ms. Pearl didn't see. He smoothed his hands down the front of his shirt and breathed deep to calm his nerves. He'd never had anyone take him home before; probably because he was always waiting for Knox. He reached for a seat across the table, but she shook her head, so he took the seat next to her instead.

She turned toward him as he sat and just looked at him for a few silent seconds while he tried very hard not to flinch.

"So," she said eventually, "I don't need to know how your relationship works. None of my business."

He smiled nervously, fighting the urge to fidget in her presence.

"Can't say I'm too shocked Billy would turn up with two lovers. That boy is greedy with love." Her smile dimmed and Santos could see echoes of worry in her gaze — years of worry Santos could relate to. "He never got enough love when he was little," she said simply, her gaze boring into his.

He nodded with a tight jaw, hating to even think about

Knox's childhood; desperate to protect a version of Knox he never even knew.

Ms. Pearl leaned forward in her seat. Her friendly face was serious but vulnerable. "That boy deserves all the love he can get. We all do. Life is already full of so much hurt, we should love and love and love whenever we can." She took her glasses from her nose so he could see her clearly. "Can you promise me that? Can you promise me he'll never feel unloved with you two?"

This trip was Santos's plan, but if he'd known how much he'd cry, he might've let the idea wither on the vine. Might. He used the back of his hands to wipe the tears from his eyes and nodded. "I can promise you that. Absolutely," he said in a voice rough with emotion.

Ms. Pearl laid her left hand on his forearm. Her thumb stroked his skin comfortingly and they sat in silence until tears stopped leaking from Santos's eyes. "Good," she whispered after a while.

A few moments later, Knox strutted from the kitchen with a bright smile on his face. He stopped at the other table and leaned on the back of Mary's chair, listening in as Marcus and Mary worked. Mary reached for Knox's hand, pulling it onto her shoulder, so she could rest her cheek against his bare forearm as if she just needed to feel his skin. Ms. Pearl nodded slowly at the scene.

They had a lot of life left to live and Santos knew neither of them would ever feel unloved, not as long as he had air in his lungs.

After a few moments, Knox looked up to make eye contact with Santos and his smile brightened. He dropped his head to whisper something in Mary's ear. She turned her gaze to Santos as Knox pulled her chair back and they made their way across the dining room. Knox pulled out the chair next to Santos and Mary slid into it. She squeezed Santos's thigh with a wink as Knox walked around the table to give Ms. Pearl a quick kiss on her cheek and take the chair on her other side.

"So what were y'all talking about?" Knox's voice was calm, but Santos thought there was a slight edge in his tone.

Ms. Pearl shifted toward him with raised eyebrows and a small smile. "I was telling your Marine that you should visit me more," she said.

Knox rolled his eyes with a laugh. "Here you go."

Ms. Pearl turned to Mary and she squeezed Santos's thigh just a little too hard. He flinched, but Mary was too focused on Ms. Pearl to notice. She sat up straight in her chair and just started blurting out words even though Ms. Pearl hadn't asked a question. "We're going to have kids. Eventually."

Ms. Pearl's face softened with a smile. "I wasn't going to ask you that, but it's good to know since Marcus" — she raised her voice and called his name loud enough to hear — "my son refuses to give me a grandchild."

"I'm single!" Marcus yelled back.

"That's why I keep sending you flyers to foster or adopt!" she yelled back.

"And I wish you would stop that, mama. I don't want to be on those listservs."

Ms. Pearl turned in her seat to fix Marcus with a glare. "You want the emails to stop? Give me a grandbaby."

Marcus sighed and pushed up from his seat. "I'm gonna check the fridge. Thanks for the recipe, Mary."

"Any time," she called back cheerily.

"If you weren't going to ask about babies, what were you going to say?" Knox asked after he stopped chuckling.

The smile Ms. Pearl gave Mary was a playful delight. "Have you considered bottling whatever got you these two men? Because honey..."

The entire table laughed.

HAPPY HOLIDAYS FROM SEA PORT

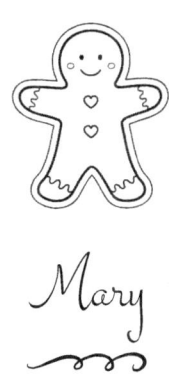

Mary

"Isn't she too old for this?" Mary asked from behind her gloved hands. "I'm too old for this."

She and Santos were standing on the sidewalk, huddled together as they watched Knox and Ms. Pearl approach a dark house without a single holiday decoration. This wasn't the best neighborhood in the city — Mary guessed from the deep potholes and flickering streetlamps more than anything else — but a few of the houses were decorated in enough holiday cheer for the whole block. They'd been visiting in the neighborhood for nearly an hour, stopping at one house or another from a list that seemed to only exist in Ms. Pearl's head, dropping off boxes of everything from wrapped presents to grocery bags of supplies for Christmas dinner.

Mary was in awe of all the personal connections Ms. Pearl and Marcus had around the city; all the people they'd helped and counted as part of their community. She was happy to be helping, but she was also freezing her nips off and trying not to complain.

"Don't let her hear you say that," Marcus laughed. "She's gonna be doing this until the day she dies, probably." He seemed used to the chill, even as soft cloudbursts of condensation erupted in the air as he spoke.

Knox was an average height, but next to Ms. Pearl, he seemed like a giant, and watching them activated a protective instinct deep inside Mary's chest. Santos threw his left arm around her shoulders and she sank into his warmth.

"Is it safe?" Santos asked, watching them like a hawk.

Mary got the distinct impression that this wasn't the first time Marcus had been asked the question by his soft laughter. "Mama's helped people all over the city, including most of the people in this neighborhood one time or another. Always when they thought they had nowhere else to go. She's probably safer here than anywhere else in the state."

Knox had woken them up before sunrise again. Santos had been grumbling about his mother at least letting them sleep in while Knox pushed him under the showerhead. He'd been much gentler coaxing Mary awake, but waking up before dawn was still waking up before dawn, no matter what filthy things he whispered in her ear.

They spent the morning at Pearl's House, sorting through donations and then packing and wrapping presents for families around the city. Christmas was still a week away, but they were making their deliveries early so families could have presents under their trees and Ms. Pearl could maximize access to three more sets of hands.

This neighborhood was only a short drive from the Strip but it looked like they were states away. Tourists came to

Vegas to live out a simulation of their wildest dreams, but this street was real life. If Santos squinted, he could see the glow from the casinos, but it wasn't enough to illuminate these streets.

Mary had been to Vegas a few times in her twenties, but in a day working with Pearl's House, she'd seen parts of the city she never even thought existed. Instead of bright, flashy hotels, there were dark, abandoned houses. Instead of paper debris advertising strip clubs and bars, there were flyers offering to buy homes at undisclosed prices. It felt far away from Sea Port's streets, but she'd seen neighborhoods like this before, just never through the eyes of people like Marcus and Ms. Pearl. The streets were still pockmarked, but Marcus knew all the kids riding their scooters around them, just like he knew the old man whose post-dinner walk included tearing down all those predatory flyers.

"Y'all look cold," Knox called as he and Ms. Pearl returned.

"We are," Mary said.

"Speak for yourself," Marcus laughed. Santos probably agreed with Marcus, but he loved Mary enough to pull her close instead of calling her out.

"One more stop," Ms. Pearl said excitedly, patting Mary on the shoulder. Marcus offered his arm to his mother and they walked ahead.

Knox stopped in front of them. "You want my scarf?"

"I'm fine," she lied.

Knox rolled his eyes and unwound the thick scarf the Santos family gave him from his neck. She was about to protest when Santos moved her between them so Knox could wrap it securely around her. Her nose filled with his cologne, making her smile.

"Better?"

She tilted her head back and offered her mouth to him as an answer. He bent forward and pressed his smile against hers. "Better," she whispered against his cool lips. It was brief but still hot, especially when the tip of his tongue tasted her bottom lip. Mary was just about to go in for more when Knox spun her around. Santos caught her at the waist and covered her mouth. He didn't bother to make her wait for some tongue.

"Better?" Knox asked, massaging her shoulders. Marcus interrupted before Mary could answer.

"Save it for later! We got work to do," Marcus yelled. Mary was surprised to find Marcus and Ms. Pearl halfway down the block. Knox and Santos offered Mary an arm each and they strolled arm-in-arm after them.

"Much, much better," she breathed happily.

SANTOS

Their last stop of the day was a grassy clearing the community had turned into a tent city. Santos's mood was somber as he tried to make sense of what he was seeing. Their small group met up with a few other volunteers Santos thought he recognized from lunch at the soup kitchen. The amount of need Santos saw was staggering and heartbreaking, but they took their cues from Ms. Pearl and Knox, who were bright-eyed and ready to get to work.

For the next couple of hours they moved in pairs, offering toiletries, extra blankets, bottled water, and flyers for the holiday meal at Pearl's House. They waded through the abandoned park from one makeshift dwelling to another, offering smiles and conversation, holding whatever sadness or anger they felt to themselves. This wasn't the time for Santos's guilt.

He kept an eye on Mary as she stopped and talked with everyone who seemed open to conversation — which was a few more people than Santos would have expected. He offered toiletries to everyone drawn to her; they turned out to be a perfect team. And even with Mary's chatty approach, they still beat Ms. Pearl and Knox back to the car.

A volunteer who introduced himself as Kevin was sorting boxes for people in need of a little more protection from the cold ground. Marcus had pulled a thermos from the back seat of his car and was offering small cups of hot tea to the other volunteers.

"Your mom is amazing," Mary said excitedly, even through chattering teeth.

Marcus searched the crowd until he spotted his mother. "You have no idea," he finally said.

"What was it like being raised by her?" Santos asked with Knox squarely on his mind.

"Fucking terrible," Marcus laughed, filling an older woman's cup with more tea. "We were always poor, no matter what. No matter how good her job or the economy or whatever, we still never had more than a couple quarters to rub together. And what little we did have, mama wanted to give away because there were always people who had even less. I hated it. Sometimes I probably even hated her, but I grew out of it eventually. She's a damn good example of how to live a good life, in my opinion."

"Yeah," Santos replied, his throat tight. Mary wrapped her arms around Santos's waist. He didn't have to wonder what she was thinking; he could feel it. One day, their kids would be just as lucky to have a father like Knox.

He coughed to clear the emotion in his throat and took a sip of his tea before turning back to the field. He found Knox and Ms. Pearl easily, slowly making their way to the curb. It was now or never. "We have something for you," Santos said.

Marcus gave him an amused smile, probably guessing what was coming since he knew Knox almost as well as they did. "What'd Billy do?"

Santos smiled while Mary rummaged in her purse, pulling out a red envelope with a bow stuck to the front.

"Knox said that sometimes donations slow down and money gets tight for the kitchen," she said, nervously licking her lips.

"We always manage," Marcus replied with an easy shrug.

"We can tell," Santos added. "But we thought that maybe sometimes when things are really tight, we could help."

"It's not a lot of money. We don't have much," Mary said, shaking the envelope between them. "But we want to help."

"She's not gonna like this," Marcus laughed.

"Knox thought that. That's why we're giving the information to the bank account we set up to you and not Ms. Pearl."

"He doesn't want me to tell her?" he asked, glancing in Knox's direction.

"Definitely not," Mary whispered.

Marcus turned to Mary. "I'll take it if you promise me something."

"My brownie recipe?" Mary asked, perking up.

Marcus considered that. "I'll take it if you promise me two things. The brownie recipe and you three come visit us more. Mama can't travel these days and even if she could, she wouldn't. But she misses Billy. We both do." When he raised his eyes to Santos, they were shiny with unshed tears.

"We can do that," Santos said, wiping at his own wet eyes. Marcus nodded gratefully.

"Take it, they're close," Mary hissed excitedly.

Marcus swiped at his eyes and plucked the envelope from Mary's hands. He turned to stuff it in the bag at his side without his mother seeing.

"Alright," Knox called when they were close. "How we feeling?"

"Cold," Mary whined.

"It's good for the circulation," Ms. Pearl laughed.

"Hungry," Santos offered.

"I know an all-day pancake place," Marcus said. "How does that sound, mama?" He extended his arm for her to hold and she held onto Knox until she was steadily in her son's care.

"Sounds like I could make pancakes at home," she replied with a smile. "But just this once, I'll let you treat me."

Marcus scoffed. "I'm not treating you, Billy is."

"Oh, well, in that case, we'll meet you there and I'll get an extra order of bacon," she said with a small pat on Knox's arm as she let Marcus lead her back to their car.

"Everything go alright?" Knox asked when they were out of earshot.

"Marcus had a counteroffer," Mary said.

"Oh, yeah?" Knox's face was bright with mischievous glee.

"He shook me down for my brownie recipe and made us promise to come and visit more often."

Knox nodded slowly and eyed her for a few seconds. "You offered the brownie recipe, didn't you?"

Santos assumed his laughter was enough of an answer to Knox's question since Mary refused to entertain the accusation.

HAPPY HOLIDAYS FROM SEA PORT

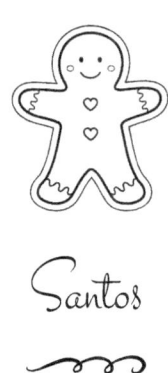

Santos

Denver was full of family, food, and relaxation. Vegas was a whirlwind of service. Ms. Pearl made sure their mornings were early and their nights were long, but they smiled more than anything else; Santos couldn't have asked for more.

It was their last night, however, and Ms. Pearl had decided to put her never-ending to-do list aside and have them over to her actual house for dinner. It was supposed to be just the three of them with Ms. Pearl and Marcus, but when they showed up at the small, tidy two-bedroom condo, they found it full of people, including many of the Pearl's House volunteers they'd been working with and a local political candidate who seemed confused but surprisingly at ease. They'd even had a few women stop by for plates before their shifts at a local strip club because there was always room for more at Pearl's table.

Over the week, Santos and Marcus had bonded over their deep practicality. When Ms. Pearl had a plan, it was

Marcus who figured out how to make it happen. Santos could relate, so he was surprised to find Marcus practically giddy while tending to his backyard smoker chock full of racks of ribs. And when he set the first plate of those ribs on the dining room table like a proud father, Santos understood why. They were the best damn ribs he'd ever tasted.

Mary and Knox were the life of the party as usual, but Santos stayed close at Ms. Pearl's side. He kept her water glass full, made her plate, and enjoyed getting to know her after years of listening to Knox's stories. After dinner, he helped her from her recliner in the living room into the kitchen. She pulled the refrigerator open and motioned toward a pan on the middle rack.

"Can you grab that for me and put it in the oven?"

Santos did as she asked.

"Woke up early to make a peach cobbler. Knox's favorite. Just gotta warm it for a bit," Ms. Pearl said, turning on the oven.

Santos pulled out a chair at the small kitchen table for Ms. Pearl to sit and she patted him on the shoulder as a thank you.

"You want something to drink?" he asked.

"Just some water. There's cold bottles in the fridge."

Santos grabbed two bottles and joined Ms. Pearl to wait for the cobbler to warm.

"Now tell me a little about your people," she said as soon as his butt hit the seat.

"I've got two little brothers," Santos started. Ms. Pearl nodded approvingly. "My parents have been together for over thirty years and they loved Knox and Mary."

That last part made her smile and nod some more. While

they waited for dessert, Santos told Ms. Pearl everything about his life that he thought his mother had asked of Mary, and she listened with warm attention. This quiet time together reminded Santos of home.

The oven dinged just as he was stumbling over how to explain his years-long crush on Knox, saving him for a few moments at least. The cobbler was bubbling and crispy when he pulled it out and set it on the stove.

"It looks good," he said.

"Of course, it does," Ms. Pearl tsk-ed. "We gotta eat it while it's hot. Take it out to the dining room, I'll grab the ice cream."

Santos took the cobbler into the dining room, holding it like a newborn baby. By the time Ms. Pearl arrived with ice cream and utensils, her guests had gathered with paper bowls in hand, ready for a scoop. They lined up on one side of the table while Santos and Ms. Pearl served them.

Knox was first in line, paper bowl cupped in his hands and the biggest smile on his face. Santos rested a scoop of vanilla ice cream on top of his cobbler. "Thank you much," Knox sang in his deepest Texas drawl, surely for no other reason than because Santos loved it.

"You're welcome." Santos said. Knox's smile shifted and he stared at him for a second too long.

"Come on, man, I'm tryna get some ice cream before my shift," Kevin said.

Knox stepped out of the way, but he kept his eyes on Santos even after he'd scooped more ice cream into waiting bowls.

It was the ice cream that tipped everyone over the edge. Before the cobbler, the party had been lively and loud. During the cobbler, the only consistent sound in the room was plastic spoons scraping every last drop from paper bowls, punctuated by Mary's happy moans while she ate. After the cobbler, there were only soft, sleepy whispers and someone's even snores. While the party succumbed to the itis, Santos stuck close to Ms. Pearl, but his gaze drifted to Knox every now and then until finally, she'd had enough.

Ms. Pearl tapped Santos's shoulder. "Go'on over there and send Mary my way."

Santos squinted in confusion.

"She's on her second helping of cobbler and she's tasting it like she's trying to work out the recipe in her head. She gave us that good biscuit recipe, it's the least I can do."

"Knox'll be happy about that," Santos said.

Ms. Pearl gave him a slow smile and a wink. "Hadn't thought about that."

Santos shook his head and walked across the living room to Mary and Knox. Knox was scraping his bowl clean while Mary was squinting at a bit of crust, lashing it with the tip of her tongue to taste the crumb. Ms. Pearl was right. Of course.

"Hey," Mary cried when she spotted Santos, finally popping the bit of crust into her mouth.

Knox swiped his tongue over his bottom lip. "You gonna hang out with us now?"

"Ms. Pearl wants to talk to you."

Mary's eyes went wide. "What'd I do?"

"Nothing. She saw you over here trying to figure out her cobbler recipe."

"Sure as hell am," Mary breathed.

"She wants to give it to— Damn, Mary!" Santos cried as she jumped from her seat and practically pushed him out the way.

"Pearl's peach cobbler, coming soon to Confections," she whispered to herself giddily as she rushed to Ms. Pearl's side.

Santos watched her walk away before turning his attention back to Knox. "You came to hang out with me, then?" Knox laughed, standing from his seat.

"Yeah," Santos breathed, licking his own lips. Knox walked to a corner of the dining room and tossed his and Mary's bowls in the trash. Santos followed, hungry for something other than cobbler.

When he was close enough, Santos bent forward and pressed his nose behind Knox's ear, the scent of his cologne filling his nostrils. Knox chuckled softly, but it was strangled and needy and it lit a fire in Santos's gut.

Knox turned to face him but stepped back as Santos stepped forward. They moved together into a dark, quiet hallway until Santos backed Knox into the wall. Their chests touched. Knox's gentle laughter caressed Santos's lips. Santos's stomach twisted into loving knots. Every breath they shared felt like electricity.

"Did you wanna kiss me under the mistletoe?"

"What mistletoe?" Santos breathed, licking the seam of Knox's smile.

Santos moved his hands to the sides of Knox's face and pulled him close, desperate all of a sudden to taste peaches on his lips.

The post-cobbler quiet broke as they kissed and the party came back to life, but Santos didn't hear any of it as he slipped his tongue into the sweeter-than-normal cavern of Knox's mouth. Knox's hands wrapped around Santos's body, his fingers kneading into his ass as he pulled Santos's jutting hips forward, grinding into Knox's hard form. They moaned together and pulled their mouths apart, gasping for air, surprised as if they hadn't been fucking one another for over a year by now.

"Fuck," Santos moaned and rested his forehead against Knox's. He was just about to go in for more when Knox shook his head.

"Not here." Knox's voice was gruff and needy as he pulled Santos deeper into the dark hallway.

"I like Ms. Pearl," Santos whispered as their bodies came together again.

Knox relaxed into Santos's hold. "I knew she'd love y'all."

"Because she loves you," Santos breathed. Knox laughed, ducking his head shyly. "Ms. Pearl made me promise to make sure that you're loved."

Knox laughed again, his hands moving to Santos's waist. "I assume you told her that's handled."

"I promised her and I'm promising you too."

"What's gotten into you?" Knox asked, rubbing Santos's back. "Where the hell is my Santos?"

He moved a hand down Knox's chest and over the front

of his jeans. Knox's breath hitched when fingers wrapped around his shaft. His eyes fluttered closed as Santos squeezed his erection through his pants.

"I'm still me," he breathed against Knox's lips, following the words' path with his tongue. "And I'm promising you that the three of us are going to be really fucking happy together. Now be quiet while I suck your dick, Sergeant."

Knox huffed out a shocked breath of laughter as Santos yanked his fly open, pushed Knox's pants down his thighs, and sank to his knees.

"Ah, there you are," Knox breathed before clamping his lips shut to stifle his moans.

Santos sucked him deep and long and slow — his favorite act of love.

HAPPY HOLIDAYS FROM SEA PORT

Knox

H e left home at eighteen. Technically, he was seventeen years, eleven months, and twenty-three days, but by the time he showed up to training, he was eighteen, and that was all that mattered. Those first few months had been disorienting. After years of planning his escape from his parents, he had to adjust to a life that was almost entirely under his own control, with hardly any guidance at all.

When he got to boot camp, he was already far more capable than some of the other men, even the ones who were older than him. His parents had been careless and neglectful, which was why Knox had learned to parent himself. He could wash and iron his own clothes, he could even mend them if he needed to, and he was a hawk with the small stash of money he'd saved before enlisting, making it last until his first paycheck — but there'd been so much about life he didn't know; so much his parents had never taught him. But the thing Knox always thought set him apart was that he never let his own inadequacies beat him down; he never let it make him cruel. He was guarded back then, but never mean, and he smiled, always open to making a friend because that's what he needed most.

But as Mary drove them toward California, the Vegas skyline disappearing in the side mirror, Knox realized that he wasn't that person anymore. Knox had lots of friends scattered all over the world, but what he wanted now — what he *needed* now — was family; *more* family. The sky was lightening rapidly behind them, but Knox's thoughts were moving faster. He'd come so far on his own, but he wanted to see where he could go now that he wasn't alone.

"How long until Berkeley?" Santos called from the back seat.

"It's eleven hours, and you know that because you planned almost every second of this trip," Mary ground out through a tight jaw.

Knox reached over the center console and grabbed her right thigh. He could feel the tension in her body, but when he squeezed her leg gently, she relaxed a little.

She forced a smile on her face. "I'm sorry."

"It's okay," Santos said quickly.

"No, it's not," Knox responded just as fast.

"It's not," Mary sighed. Knox watched her look in the rearview mirror and she tried to smile. "I'm sorry, I'm just tense."

"We know," Knox said.

"As long as we don't take any detours or long breaks, we should arrive before it gets too dark."

Knox slipped his hand between her thighs. "Sounds boring," he whispered with a smile.

"Cool it," Santos grunted. "I don't want to die in a car crash because you can't keep it in your pants."

"I'm an excellent driver," Mary said, finally smiling for real.

"Yeah, you are." Knox turned in his seat and smirked. "And if I didn't plan to keep it in my pants, I'd be in the back seat with you."

Santos grunted, but Mary let out a lovely peal of laughter. Knox winked at Santos before turning back around in his seat.

"So, how are we playing this?" Knox asked, squeezing Mary's thigh again.

"What do you mean?"

Knox took a few seconds to consider his words. He wanted to keep this conversation as light as possible. "I mean you're clearly tense about us meeting your mother, so what do you want us to know? What do you want us not to do or say?"

Knox didn't like having to tiptoe around anything with Mary; he loved her too much. They were normally direct with one another, but this leg of the trip seemed to be chipping away little pieces of Mary's self-confidence and he felt like he was watching her fold into herself, one tiny bit at a time. Knox didn't want that for her but he couldn't stop it, so he handled her with the gentlest touch.

"My parents separated a few months ago," Mary said. "My dad had to tell me because my mom won't even talk about it with me."

"Is that abnormal?" Knox asked. "Her not telling you things, I mean."

Mary shook her head and laughed drily. "Par for the fucking course," she bit out.

As someone who grew up in a home that was one big minefield, Knox knew better than to rush her.

"I was still hoping my dad would be around so y'all could meet him, but he's...not."

"He doesn't want to meet us?" Santos asked in a voice as careful as Knox's.

She shook her head quickly. "I don't know. I haven't been able to get him on the phone for more than a few minutes. Whatever's going on with him and my mother, he's just...I don't know...hiding out. He sent me an email a few days ago telling me he was going fishing with my uncle Ronnie. He said he made the plans before he knew I was coming. I don't know if I believe that, but it is what it is."

"Email?" Knox asked.

"Yeah," Mary breathed, pressing her lips together in frustration. Knox squeezed her thigh again. "So it'll just be my mom y'all are gonna meet."

"No other family?" Knox asked carefully.

"Oh. Actually, no, you're right," she laughed, smiling again. "Some of my aunts and cousins should be at her house for Christmas dinner. You'll meet them too. They'll be good. Well, they'll be themselves, just regular family weird."

"Okay, good," Knox said.

Knox knew Mary loved her mother, but it was clear that loving her didn't make any of this easy. If anything, the years of their dysfunctional relationship had become a liability to her happiness. She could see it, but she didn't know what to do with that reality, and it wasn't his place to tell her. Loving her mother from afar was easy, but even the possibility of loving her up close had been hanging over her head this entire trip like a rain cloud, spoiling even the best moments they'd shared.

Knox snuck a glance at Santos, who was sitting in the middle of the back seat, fists clenched in his lap, letting Knox take the lead on this conversation. They wanted to be there for her, but the guardrails Mary had erected around her feelings were impossibly high.

"Does your mom know about us?" Knox asked. "Do you want us to say we're just friends?"

"No!" Mary didn't normally yell. Well, she didn't normally yell when they weren't having sex, so this caught them all off guard. "I'm sorry."

"Don't apologize," Knox said, squeezing her thigh again.

She glanced at him with pained eyes. "I don't want to lie about our relationship. I'd never ask you to do that. She already knows about us."

"Okay," Knox breathed. Santos contributed another grunt.

"My mother is judgmental as hell. All my life, no decision I've ever made has been good enough for her. No school I got into was elite enough. No accolade I received was prestigious enough. She's always made me feel like *I* was never enough. Like I wasn't living up to my potential. Eventually, I just stopped telling her things. If it wouldn't affect my relationship with her, I kept it to myself. I didn't tell her I got denied tenure until I was moving to Sea Port. Like, on the way. It's just easier to deal with her that way. And when it came to my life in Sea Port, I gave her the bare minimum of information, most on bakery treats and Catleen."

"Cat-leen does have a lot going on," Knox offered.

She was too tense to laugh, but she managed a smile.

"What'd she say about us?" Knox asked.

"Nothing, really."

Santos exhaled loudly, the tension from the back seat a palpable thing.

"What does 'nothing, really' mean, sweetheart?" Knox asked. If she kept chewing her lips, Knox thought they'd be raw by the time they made it to California.

"My mother's the kind of person who thinks avoiding difficult things is polite. Harmony is more important than honesty. So, when I told her about you two, she just...asked if I wanted her to make gumbo." Mary had the steering wheel in a chokehold.

Knox was trying his hardest to keep it cool, but this wasn't what he expected at all. "Hold on. You told your mother you're dating two men and she doesn't have *anything* to say about it?"

"Nothing," Mary said, letting out a long, frustrated sigh.

When Knox glanced at Santos again, the other man looked just as bewildered as Knox felt.

"Even my parents had questions," Santos said. "They asked if we were in a cult." He was too tense to laugh, so Knox did it for him.

"Can three people be a cult?" she asked.

"It's enough to start one," Santos offered thoughtfully.

"Let's stay on track," Knox said, cutting this conversational detour off at the knees. Mary and Santos grumbled, and he sighed. "We can talk about that later."

"Fine," Mary replied testily.

"Do you know why your mama's feeling like this?" Knox asked carefully. "Is there any way we can make this easier on you, her, everyone involved?"

The car was silent for a while. Knox caressed her thigh, waiting for Mary to speak without pressure.

Finally, Mary shrugged. "I don't know. I love my mother, but sometimes I feel like I don't really understand her. This is just what she does. She ignores the things she doesn't like. If you try to get her to work through the issue, she makes you feel like you're the problem. She'll nitpick me and then be disappointed that I'm not more confident. She'll judge every decision I make and then act surprised when I don't tell her anything." After the rush of those words, Mary took a deep breath and then let it out with a small growl. Somehow, her knuckles tightened around the steering wheel.

Knox shifted back over the center console at the same time as Santos undid his seatbelt and leaned forward, crowding the space between their front seats.

"Alright," Knox said carefully. "Now that we know that, how do you want to play this?"

"What do you mean?"

Santos answered first. "We're in this together."

"We are," Knox echoed. "If this is how your mother behaves, then so be it. This trip isn't about changing her. It's not even really about her, it's about us."

"And our relationship," Santos added seriously.

"So we need a game plan that protects what really matters," Knox said.

"What really matters?" Mary asked in a small, shaky, hopeful voice.

"Us," Knox and Santos replied at the same time. That one word brought an immediate smile to her face.

For the first time in this conversation, Mary's shoulders relaxed. Knox saw her eyes shining with tears before she blinked them away, but one fell over her cheek. Santos reached from the back seat and brushed his thumb over that wet streak as soon as it fell. His hand landed atop of Knox's, settling heavily on Mary's thigh.

"I want to play it by ear," she eventually said. "I know we're thinking of staying a week, but maybe we... Maybe I'll feel better if we don't have to stay so long? If we can leave if it gets to be too much?" She asked those questions in a small squeak.

"We'll stay for as little or as long as you want," Knox answered softly.

"I'm sorry," she whispered.

"Don't apologize," Santos said gruffly. Knox turned to him with raised eyebrows. "I mean you don't have anything to apologize for," he amended.

"You say the word and we're outta there," Knox agreed. "We can be home in no time."

"Home," Mary echoed in a wistful whisper that broke Knox's heart.

Santos squeezed Knox's hand and Knox squeezed her thigh. They stayed like that for a few seconds, arms tangled together across the center console.

Eventually, Santos sat back and buckled his seatbelt again. Knox shoved his sunglasses onto his face now that the sun was glaring off the side mirrors, but he put his hand back on Mary's thigh.

"So what should we name our cult?" Knox asked.

Mary's laugh was a thin breath of air, nothing like the loud cackle Knox had come to adore, but it would do for now.

HAPPY HOLIDAYS FROM SEA PORT

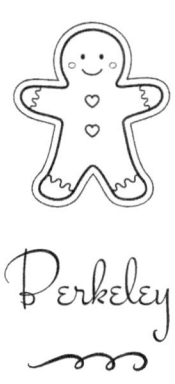

Perkeley

KNOX

Mary was asleep in the back seat by the time they made it to her hometown.

Knox was at the wheel, creeping along a residential street while Santos was half-hanging out of the passenger window, squinting at the house numbers in the dark. They didn't want to wake Mary, but the GPS kept telling them they had arrived — but where?

Her friend Dominique had offered her home for their stay, but they didn't know what her house looked like and none of the addresses were visible from the street. Knox was getting frustrated, but Santos was already there.

"Pull over, I'm gonna steal her phone," Santos whispered.

"It's locked and she's asleep."

"I can put her finger on the sensor without waking her up," he replied, already turning toward the back seat.

Knox eased his foot onto the brake. "So we're just gonna run a heist on our girlfriend's phone now?" he laughed.

"Better that than we just keep riding around in circles some more. My ass is killing me. Don't make a joke out of that, I'm not in the mood."

Knox laughed softly as he slowed the car along the curb. He shifted the gearshift to park and turned on the overhead light. Santos was already leaning into the back seat.

With the light on, Knox could see Mary was flat on her back with her phone clutched against her chest. Santos's fingers were wrapped around Mary's phone when he stopped.

"Mmhmm," Knox hummed.

"Shut up," Santos hissed and moved his hand from her phone to her shoulder. "Mary." Santos whispered her name as if he wasn't fully committed to waking her up. He probably wasn't.

"You're gonna have to say her name louder than that." It was true, but he just liked to antagonize Santos.

"She looks peaceful, though."

"She ain't gonna look peaceful if she finds out you busted into her phone."

"I just need the address," Santos shot back defensively.

Knox sucked his teeth. "We already have the address. We just don't know which house is which. You just don't want her to be annoyed that you woke her up."

"And if I don't?" Their car was dark, but Knox had a decent view of Santos's face in the glare from a streetlight and it was harsh. The pain etched into the lines of his face took all Knox's enjoyment out of the moment.

Knox smoothed the back of his hand over Santos's stubbly cheek. "You gotta get over it," he whispered. "That fight was weeks ago. You gotta stop treating her like she's made of glass. You two can be mad at each other sometimes. It's not gonna break us."

Those words had been on Knox's heart for weeks, just waiting for the right time; waiting for the moment when Santos was ready to hear them. If Mary was hurting, they all were. If Santos was stressed, they all were. And if Mary and Santos were at odds, Knox felt like he was being pulled apart.

Santos pressed his cheek against the back of Knox's hand. "I'm worried she's gonna blame me if the trip isn't perfect. I'm terrified she'll hate me," he whispered.

Knox huffed out a soft breath. "Your dick was literally touching the back of her throat this morning. If that's hate, then she can hate me forever," he said, laughing so hard his stomach hurt.

"Shh," Santos hissed. "And that...it's different for me."

"Explain," Knox said.

"I'm not like you two."

"Black?" Knox laughed. "We know."

Santos rolled his eyes. "It's easy for you two to just... smile and flirt with everybody."

"It's a gift," Knox chuckled.

"You two are lucky," Santos breathed. "Everybody loves you. It's easy to love you two."

Knox's laughter gentled until it died. He scrutinized Santos's face and he didn't like what he saw — discomfort and fear warring in his eyes. "Meaning you think it's hard to love you?" Knox tried not to sound like a drill sergeant, but he refused to let this stand.

"Harder than you two," Santos hedged.

"I used to dream about being loved by...anyone," Knox said carefully. "I used to wonder how I had two parents and felt like an orphan. Love's never come easy to me. Not until you two."

Santos's jaw clenched for a few seconds before he relaxed his head against the headrest. "I was so damn mad at her," he finally said. "And I didn't even want to be. All I could think when we were yelling at each other was that she was going to realize that three people is too hard. And if she had to choose, she'd definitely choose you."

Knox's heart was pounding a happy beat against his chest and he chuckled softly, but his breath was thin. "I don't know if you don't remember or if you're just being stupid, but she literally had the chance to choose one of us and refused."

"That was at the beginning, though. Things could change."

"Nothing seemed to change as of last night if I remember correctly."

"What about you?" Santos asked.

"What about me? I'm perfect. You two are never mad at me," he laughed.

Santos reached for Knox's hand and their fingers tangled together. "Do you think three is too hard?"

"I think the three of us makes me hard," he chuckled before kissing the back of Santos's hand. "I think the three of us are perfect as we are. There ain't nowhere else I'd rather be. No other people I wanna be with."

"Preach," Mary yawned. They startled at her voice and Knox pressed the dome light to find Mary stretching along the length of the back seat.

"How long have you been up?" Knox laughed.

"Since before you got off the freeway."

Knox sucked his teeth. "And you've just been laying back there while we drove around in circles?"

Mary sat up with a smug smile. "I'd have told you eventually, but you two were so confused and mad. It was cute."

She leaned between the front seats and turned her full attention to Santos. When she spoke, she used her sweetest voice. "Just let the fight go, babe. You're never getting rid of me."

She turned to Knox next. "And for the record, you piss me off at least once a day."

"Bullshit," Knox laughed.

Mary let out an exasperated sigh and scooted toward the door. "Come on, we're here."

"Where?" Knox and Santos cried at the same time.

HAPPY HOLIDAYS FROM SEA PORT

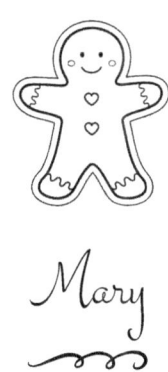

Mary

They unpacked the car and went straight to bed — no funny business, just sleep.

The next morning, Mary woke up first and climbed over Knox to get out of bed. She tiptoed from the room, trying not to wake them.

She hadn't been to Dom's house since the house-warming party, but it barely looked like the small fixer-upper she remembered. Dom had been in her DIY bag for the last year and a half, changing out fixtures and hardware, even painting a few walls. She'd seen pictures in their friend group chat, but now that she was seeing all her friend's hard work in person, she was really proud of her.

She was also nosy as hell. Mary wasn't even fully awake before she started rifling through Dom's kitchen. She opened every cabinet and drawer, she flung Dom's refrigerator open and looked through every shelf. Hell, she was about to do the same in the freezer when Knox cleared his throat.

She froze, head in the fridge, before turning around to find him in a pair of boxers and nothing else. He was standing sentry at the kitchen entrance, arms crossed over his chest — his big, beautiful, naked chest.

"Something going on here?" he asked in a dry voice.

Mary reached for a bottle of water from the fridge. "Nope," she said, closing the refrigerator door. "Just getting something to drink."

He watched her twist open the cap and take a deep swig. Knox was also barely awake as she sauntered toward him.

"Nothing, huh?" he said, eyes, dipping to her hips. Mary offered Knox the bottle of water and waited until he grabbed it from her hand. "So you're just ransacking your friend's kitchen for nothing?" he asked, smiling around the bottle.

Mary smirked but watched Knox drink, licking her lips as his Adam's apple bobbed. "We're friends," she whispered. "This is friendship."

Knox offered Mary the bottle again. He drank more than half, so Mary finished it off. When she was done, Knox snatched the bottle back, crushed it, and dropped it into the recycle bin next to the trash can. "Friendship, huh?"

"Yep. I just want to make sure things are okay. You know, that she has enough food in the pantry, the right kind of hot sauce, stuff like that."

"Invading her privacy," Knox said.

Mary grabbed the kettle and moved to the sink. "Her pantry isn't private," she corrected.

Knox approached behind her, hands on her hips as he molded his body against her back, rubbing his groin against her ass. "So you're gonna stop here then?" he asked, his lips kissing the sensitive skin in the crook of her neck.

"You want coffee?"

He moved them to the coffee station on the counter like they were one organism.

"Yes," he whispered while kissing his way across her shoulder. "And I'm gonna take that as a yes."

Mary had a smart reply on her tongue, but Knox was touching her soft stomach and kissing her neck and it was all she could do to focus on loading the ground coffee into the French press.

And the worst part was that he knew what he was doing to her and she could feel how much he liked it. As soon as she turned the machine on, Knox started pulling her t-shirt over her hips, but then Santos cleared his throat. Mary felt Knox's smile against her pulse.

"Good morning, Santos," she said. Maybe moaned.

"Is there coffee?" he asked.

"Making it now." She definitely moaned this time.

Santos appeared at her side and pressed his body against them, brushing his mouth against her cheek. "Thanks."

"How'd you..." Mary's voice fell apart because Knox had managed to pull her shirt up to her waist and pushed her panties over her hips until they fell to her ankles. Cool air hit her pussy for a second and Mary had to take a breath before she felt comfortable speaking again. "How'd you sleep?" she finally managed. She got those words out as Knox pulled his dick from his boxers and rubbed his shaft between her legs. She let out a high-pitched moan and squirmed as the delicious friction of his softest skin against hers took her breath away.

Santos leaned his hip against the counter and started caressing her breasts through her shirt while Knox rocked between her thighs, the head of his shaft bumping against her clit.

"I slept like a damn log," Santos said. "How 'bout you?"

A soft whimper was all she could offer at the moment.

"And you?" he asked Knox.

"I slept alright," he panted against Mary's skin, rocking his hips back and forth. "What are we gonna do today?"

Mary's thighs clenched around Knox's shaft as a tremor moved through her. Knox grunted into her neck while Santos rolled her nipple between his fingers. "That's an option. We could also do a little sightseeing later."

Mary was listening, she was comprehending, but she was also getting wet.

"Any ideas?" Knox asked before sucking her earlobe into his mouth.

"Yes," Mary moaned, not because she had any ideas but because the head of Knox's dick brushed against her opening.

"Where?" Santos asked, palming her other breast in his free hand.

"Fuck," she whimpered. Knox's laughter made her clit jump and she moaned low and deep.

Santos squeezed her breasts. "I used to serve with this guy who loved the Asian Art Museum. It's in San Francisco, though."

Knox released her ear from his mouth and moved back. Mary whimpered weakly as his hand landed between her shoulders and pushed her forward. She lost Santos's hands on her breasts for a second so he could pull her shirt up and over her head. Knox smoothed his hand down her spine and eased inside of her with his full length.

Mary tried to keep track of the plans they were making. She wanted to offer suggestions, there were so many places she wanted to take them, but Knox was fucking her slow and deep while Santos fondled her breasts, so it was hard to concentrate. Even harder to concentrate when Knox pulled out to let Santos replace him inside her pussy. Whatever their plans for the day, they wouldn't start until after their mid-morning nap and the coffee would have to go to waste.

What a great way to start the day, though!

SANTOS

They spent the afternoon in The City, walking around downtown, visiting Mary's favorite museums, and enjoying the warm winter day. They finished it all off with a train ride to the Mission for burritos before heading back to Dominique's house to relax.

They were almost as tired as the night before, but now that Santos had gotten a few hours' sleep, he could appreciate the details of the neighborhood, like the sad state of Dominique's holiday decorations. Dominique's house was a wood shingle bungalow with a wide porch and a red front door. The neighborhood was neat and welcoming, but Dom's sad decorations were bringing the block down. One of her neighbors had a full-on Santa on a sleigh with half a dozen reindeer on their lawn, but all Dominique had was a single string of multicolored lights hanging off the front of the roof. They weren't even straight.

"No offense, Mary, but your friend's decorations are sad," Santos breathed. Knox choked back a sharp laugh.

"Dom's an atheist," Mary replied testily, unclasping her seatbelt with a little more energy than was necessary. "The neighborhood association is trying to impose 'aesthetic uniformity,' so this is her pushback. So is the Santa scene. I think."

"I hate HOAs," Knox said.

"It's not even an HOA," Mary cried. "That's why everyone's pissed."

They climbed from the car. "Don't tell her I talked about her decorations," Santos pleaded.

"I'm definitely telling her," she laughed.

"Mary—"

"She won't care. Besides, I told her to get a light-up kinara for Kwanzaa, but she didn't want to listen to me."

"Wow," was all Knox said as he led the way to the front door.

"I think it would've been cute," Mary mumbled, grabbing Santos's hand.

"Where is she?" Santos asked once they made their way inside.

Knox flipped on the living room light and they kicked their shoes off at the door.

"She unofficially moved in with her boyfriend a few months ago."

"Unofficially?" Knox asked.

They congregated in the kitchen. Santos was paying attention, but he was also having flashbacks to this morning.

His stomach clenched and his dick hardened, but he tried to ignore it.

Mary opened the fridge with a shrug. "It's a trial run. If they break up or he's too messy, she'll move back here. Until then, she rents the place to visiting faculty on a short-term basis to cover her mortgage. Her new tenant doesn't arrive until after the new year."

"I like her. She sounds practical," Santos said, eyeing the bottle of wine Mary pulled from the fridge.

"You would say something like that," Knox breathed, smiling brightly when Santos glared in his direction.

Mary's phone chimed, so she handed the bottle to Santos and moved to the couch to dig around in her purse. Knox started pulling open drawers, looking for a bottle opener, while Mary frowned down at her phone.

"You okay?" Santos asked. It took a few seconds for Mary to respond and it was only to shake her head.

"Talk to us, sweetheart," Knox said gently before snatching the bottle from Santos's hands and opening it.

Her fingers were flying over the phone screen for a few moments before exhaling loudly. "It's my mom," she said, brows bunched together. They'd had the loveliest day but all the happiness he'd seen on Mary's face was wiped away.

"What's she saying?" Knox asked.

"She asked if we made it."

Her phone chimed again and Mary's face flinched. "And she wants us to come to the Christmas Eve gathering at her church." She chewed her bottom lip while reading from her phone.

"Is that a good thing?" Santos asked carefully.

Mary shook her head, typing quickly before tossing it

haphazardly onto the couch. She closed her eyes and exhaled loudly before turning back to them, a forced smile on her beautiful mouth. "I have no idea. Wanna see if we can all fit into Dom's shower?"

"No," Knox said definitively.

Mary's shoulders slumped in sadness.

"We can take showers separately and then go to bed. To sleep," he added with emphasis. "You don't have to talk about what you're feeling if you're not ready, but I'm not about to let you use our dicks to avoid a serious conversation."

She glared at him for a few seconds before turning to Santos. "You gonna let him speak for you?"

Santos opened his mouth but Knox cut him off. "He is. And if he wants to use my mouth, I'll let him."

Santos's eyes bounced between Mary and Knox, feeling a little trapped and a lot horny at the same time. He could see her brain working while she glared at them, but Knox was at ease, uncorking the wine bottle as if he didn't have a care in the world. Meanwhile, Santos's stomach felt like there was popcorn popping in his gut. He hated when they fought, even if he wasn't really in the disagreement.

"You sure you want to do this?" Mary asked.

"Do what?" Knox replied, punctuating the question with a sharp pop as he pulled the cork free.

"Antagonize me."

Santos's heart was pounding against his chest, but Knox just smiled as he put the wine opener back in the drawer by the sink.

"Is that what I'm doing, sweetheart?" Knox glanced in her direction with an easy smile. He even had the nerve to wink at her because Knox was...well, Knox. Santos couldn't imagine doing that. In fact, his fingers were wrapped around the counter in an iron grip.

"Yes," she said, but her voice was reedy and weak.

Knox opened one and then another cabinet, looking for wine glasses, while Mary was worrying her bottom lip in the living room. Santos was torn between them, wanting to wrap Mary in his arms and take Knox up on his offer. He had no idea what to do, so he did nothing, hating the way it made him feel.

Knox found three mismatched wine glasses with cheerful phrases like 'cheers' and 'pour one out' written on the sides and set them next to the wine bottle before resting his palms on the counter and finally meeting her gaze.

"Ms. Pearl used to tell me that when someone pokes us where we're tender, we lash out in anger, but at the bottom of all that was usually just more pain."

When Santos turned his gaze back to Mary, she was still worrying her bottom lip, but her eyes were shimmering with tears. "I don't want to talk about it," she whispered.

"And you don't have to," Knox said again. "Just like I don't have to pretend like sex fixes everything."

"It can fix a lot," Mary whispered. Santos grunted softly because she had a point.

Even Knox had to laugh. "Well, you got me there, but this ain't one of those things. Not if you claim to love us."

Those last few words hit Santos as hard as Mary. "I do love you." Her bottom lip quivered as she spoke.

"And we love you too."

"We do," Santos said, finally feeling comfortable enough to speak.

"See?" Knox laughed. "He can speak for himself. What are you feeling, sweetheart? What's got you tender?"

Mary and Santos opened their mouths at the same time.

"Grow up," he sighed, rolling his eyes.

They waited in silence, even though it was killing Santos. Mary's eyes shimmered with tears and her nose flared with every breath as she tried not to let them fall. The only reason Santos didn't rush across the small living room to hug her was because of Knox. His face and body were relaxed, but Santos could feel the tidal wave of tension wafting off him.

If Knox could keep it together, so could he.

Mary finally lost the battle with her tears and they fell over the lovely curve of her full cheeks. She swiped at her wet face angrily. "I don't know what's going to happen tomorrow. I'm scared," she whispered. "I'm terrified she'll say or do something that'll ruin...us."

"She can't," Knox said at the same time Santos grunted, "Not gonna happen."

"You say that now."

"I can say it tomorrow too if you want," Knox said. "We can say it as many times as you like. You know I love to talk."

Santos grunted out a harsh laugh and Mary smiled, wiping more tears from her face.

"I love you two," she said.

"And we love you," Knox replied for him and Santos.

"I just want... I just want to feel safe tonight before all hell breaks loose."

"Oh, that's it?" Knox asked, barking out a laugh. He grabbed the wine bottle and filled one glass after another. "We can do that for sure. You wanna sit on Santos's face?"

Mary burst into shocked laughter as Santos glared in Knox's direction.

"What? We all know how you prefer to use your mouth."

Santos rolled his eyes but didn't refute Knox's claim.

"You wanna keep talking or do you wanna suck on her clit?"

Santos grabbed a glass of wine and took an annoyed gulp.

"So, you gonna answer him or...?" Mary whispered.

"That's our girl," Knox laughed, grabbing the other glasses of wine. He walked into the living room and handed one to Mary. She took the glass but offered her mouth to him instead of drinking. Santos took another sip of his wine while Mary and Knox kissed one another. He watched, sipping his wine serenely, while the blood and liquor rushed to his groin. Knox was right.

He usually was.

HAPPY HOLIDAYS FROM SEA PORT

Christmas Eve

KNOX

Knox woke up first, but he was trapped under Santos's heavy ass arm. Instead of fighting his iron grip, Knox stared at the ceiling for a few minutes until he had to pee. He slipped off the side and grabbed one of Santos's sweatshirts from the foot of the bed, rushing from the bedroom as quietly as possible. The rest of the house was much colder and he slipped the sweater over his head and started making coffee, feeling bleary-eyed and deliciously sore. He filled the kettle sitting on the stove and waited in exhausted silence for it to boil. He'd just poured the boiling water into the French press when the front door unlocked and opened. Knox's reflexes were slow, so he just watched as a tall, dark-skinned woman with black and red braids down to her waist strutted inside.

She took a few steps into the living room before she noticed Knox standing in the kitchen watching her. She froze and they stared at each other in confusion or shock or disbelief.

"Good morning," he rasped.

"Good morning."

"Are you Dominique?"

She shook her head. "I'm Keisha. Are you Knox?"

He was just awake enough to smile. "I am. It's nice to finally meet you."

"You as well," she said, closing the front door behind her and kicking off her shoes. "Dom gave me her key so I could come check on you three."

"Check on us?"

She walked toward him with a smirk. "I think she was worried y'all might break her bed."

Knox let out an involuntary laugh and shook his head. He was awake enough to finally greet her, offering his hand to shake as they met in the small walkway. "I shoulda expected something like that from one of Mary's friends."

"Two," she corrected, accepting his offer. She smiled for a few seconds before her eyes narrowed and she squeezed his hand in an adorable attempt to intimidate him. "Do you love her?" Keisha asked, watching him closely.

The question might have caught him off-guard a few weeks ago, but after so many straightforward introductions during this trip, Knox felt like a pro and didn't miss a beat. "We do. We love her a whole damn lot."

She watched him for a few seconds before nodding once and smiling again. "Good," she trilled. "She deserves it."

Now that the friendly intimidation was done, Keisha looked Knox over from head to toe. He wasn't prepared for this. He'd just climbed out of bed, for God's sake, and wasn't even shirtless. Keisha didn't seem to mind, though.

"I know that's right, girl," Keisha mumbled to herself.

"Alright, that's enough," Knox laughed.

"My bad. So where is she?"

He gestured toward the bedroom door. "They're still knocked out."

"You guys must be tired. After your road trip, I mean."

"Sure," he laughed, walking back into the kitchen.

She set her purse on the coffee table and checked her watch, chewing her bottom lip.

"Is something going on? Something I don't know about?"

"I don't want you guys to be late," she started to say when the door creaked open again.

The woman who walked into the house was Keisha's complete opposite. She was short and thin with light brown skin. She had a short, dyed honey-blonde curly afro tapered at the sides with reindeer antlers on a headband bouncing as she walked. She was also wearing a long Christmas-themed sweater dress with a ribbon belt tied at her waist and a pair of high-heeled knee-high boots.

"Ho, ho, ho, let's do the damn thing!"

Keisha let out a frustrated breath of air. "You are so embarrassing."

"And you are so repressed these days. Hi, I'm Leah," the new woman called to Knox. "And you are absolutely Knox." Her eyes wandered appreciatively up and down his body.

"How'd you know?"

"I stalk the Confections and Sea Port social media," she said proudly. "Where's Santos?"

"And Mary?" Keisha added.

"Uh, yeah, yeah. Her too. Can't wait to see her or whatever."

Knox felt a chuckle building in his throat when the bedroom door opened.

"What's going on out— OH MY GOD!" Mary screamed and then her friends joined her in the screaming.

Knox flinched at the volume of their shrieking. The women were jumping and yelling and hugging like a manic coven performing a ritual. Santos appeared in the doorway and he yawned before finding Knox's eyes.

Sleep and confusion warred on Santos's face, but above all that was happiness.

This was the Mary they knew and loved.

They climbed out of the car in front of a Baptist church that had seen better days — better decades, even. Knox had never been religious, but he recognized an old building when he saw one.

"This it?" Santos asked, even though the GPS had answered that question already.

Mary nodded but didn't speak. She was too busy staring up at the building with worried eyes.

The morning sky had been crisp and clear, but now it was a moody shade of blue, thick pockets of clouds obscuring the sun. The weather reminded Knox of an early spring day in Sea Port and he had the urge to be there, just for a moment so he could breathe without all the tension clogging the air between them. He'd been all in favor of the trip, but it had been an emotional rollercoaster and it was starting to wear on him. As much as he'd cherished these past few weeks, he also couldn't wait to get home to the life they were building.

"Calm down," he whispered directly into Mary's ear, smoothing his fingers over the hand clenched at her side. "It'll be just fine."

"You don't know that," she said in a broken whisper.

Santos stood on Mary's other side, protecting her. "We'll be fine as long as we're together."

"Oh my goodness, I need to get a picture of this," Leah squealed as she and Keisha stepped in front of them. "Turn to me."

Leah took the picture before they could truly register what she'd said. "Okay, now one with more smiles and less what the fuck," she said, snapping above her phone.

"Don't cuss in front of the church," Keisha hissed.

After she took the picture, Leah turned to her friend. "I can't cuss *outside* the church? Is this a new rule?"

Knox and Santos chuckled but Mary was too busy fidgeting to join them. Knox pulled her hands apart and laced their fingers together.

"Maybe this was a bad idea," she said.

Keisha pursed her lips in consideration but Leah rushed forward. "Bad or not, incoming."

They turned toward the church in unison. Knox would've recognized Mary's mother immediately; they were the spitting image of one another.

"Our kids are going to have the best genes," Santos said.

"Oh shit. Are you pregnant?" Keisha whipped her head around.

Mary's shoulders relaxed and she rolled her eyes, pulling

her hand from Knox's grasp and balling her fists on her hips. "If one more fucking person asks me about my uterus."

"Apparently, you're not supposed to cuss outside of the church now, so…" Leah offered. Keisha rolled her eyes at that.

"Mary."

They all stood straighter at the stern voice. Knox had never heard Mary's name said with so little joy.

"Mary Lynette." She stopped next to Keisha, but everyone else who wasn't Mary might as well have been see-through.

"H-hi, mama." There was a moment of hesitation before Mary finally took a step forward. Her mother's face was blank and her back was stiff, but she opened her arms as Mary approached.

Mary was a hugger. She liked to hug Santos, Knox, Bria, her favorite customers, her least favorite customers, the post-woman when she came in with a cart full of packages. She'd once even managed to hug an entire preschool class while keeping a hot pot of caramel out of their reach. If someone was within arm's length, they were in the hugging zone, but when she stepped into her mother's arms, it was the stiffest embrace Knox had ever seen. The fact that Mary couldn't find a way to hug her own mother with any warmth broke his heart and for the first time, he second-guessed this trip.

Their embrace only lasted for a few seconds and as soon as it ended, Mary started fidgeting again. Knox couldn't blame her; he would've fidgeted under her disapproving glare as well. But still, her mother only had eyes for Mary.

"Have you gained weight?" she said in a sharp tone that took all the air from their lungs.

"Um... I..." Mary cleared her throat nervously. "Mama, this is, um, this is Santos and Knox. They're my—"

"Yes," her mother snapped. "I received your text message. There's no need to repeat it, especially not here."

Knox could smile in almost any situation, it was his gift, but this was one of those elusive moments when he couldn't even pull his mouth into a smirk. Instead, his jaw tightened and he stepped closer to Mary's side. He could feel fury radiating from Santos's body, but they did their best to keep it from showing on their faces.

"Hey, Mrs. Woods," Keisha said in a bright tone, pulling her attention from Mary. "How are you?"

Her face practically lit up when her gaze landed on Keisha. She seemed like a totally different person, like the kind of person who'd never eviscerate her daughter's self-esteem in a sentence simply because she could. Knox wanted to get to know the version of Mary's mother Keisha was getting.

"Keisha Parker. I'm doing well. Aren't you lovely?" She looked Keisha over from head-to-toe, nodding approvingly.

Knox felt Mary's body tighten and he moved his hand to the small of her back.

Leah's reception was less warm. Actually, it was only two words. "Leah Gordon," she ground out before turning back in Mary's direction, and they all flinched.

"I told the First Lady you'd be here today and she wants to see you. It's been so long since you've been back," she said, each word full of judgment. She spared Knox and Santos a withering glance. "I'd prefer if we didn't share your...relationship status. I don't mind what you all do behind closed doors," she said in a tone of voice that indicated she definitely did mind, "but there's no need to talk about it in the house of the Lord."

Before Knox or Santos could respond, she grabbed Mary's arm and pulled her toward the church. Mary glanced over her shoulder with sad, apologetic eyes while Knox and Santos stood there in shock.

Knox's heart was pounding an angry rhythm against his chest. The farther away Mary got, the more Knox felt like he was living in a terrible alternate universe than the rest of the trip.

"Well, congratulations," Leah said brightly. "You've survived meeting the ice queen."

"It probably doesn't seem like it," Keisha shrugged, "but that wasn't that bad."

"What?" Knox drawled.

"It could've been so much worse," Keisha said.

"How?" Santos asked through gritted teeth.

Keisha and Leah shrugged in unison. "She could've ignored you completely," Keisha offered nonchalantly.

"She's done it before," Leah added. "It was awkward as fuck."

Knox wanted to argue that might have been better, but complaining wouldn't get them anywhere, so he pressed his lips shut and trained his eyes on Mary's tense back as she moved further and further away.

HAPPY HOLIDAYS FROM SEA PORT

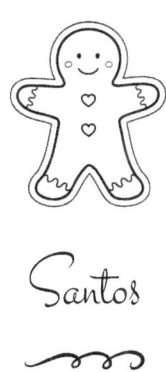

Santos

~~

Knox and Santos staked out a table in the corner, clear across the room from Mary. Knox seemed calm and friendly, but Santos was seething. This wasn't how he hoped they would spend their Christmas Eve at all.

For the last hour, Mary's mother had done her best to keep Mary far away from her friends — except Keisha — ever since she'd dragged her inside the building. She led Mary around the church's rec room, stopping at nearly every table re-introducing her to the other congregants, showing her off like a prize pony. Santos had assumed Mary would trot him and Knox around like *her* prize ponies. He was prepared to suffer through that, but this was real torture.

Leah approached them with a friendly smile, two plastic cups of grape juice in one hand and a plate of snacks in the other. She set everything on the table in front of them. "You two look pissed," she said, a look of playful pity written all over her face.

"We are," Santos breathed, hating that this was ruining their first meeting with Mary's friends in person.

"Him especially," Knox added with a wink. Santos glared for a few seconds before offering a small smile.

"There you go," Knox whispered, coaxing Santos into a slightly bigger smile.

Leah dropped into a chair at their table. The pitying look had at least disappeared. "This is even cuter in person. I'm loving this for our girl."

"Thanks," Santos ground out.

"Don't mind him," Knox said, squeezing his shoulder. "Is her mother ever going to let us near her?"

Leah's smile faltered for a second before she shook her head. "Probably not. I'm sorry. I doubt it's personal."

"Feels pretty damn personal to me," Santos said.

Leah turned and looked over her shoulder and Santos's eyes went immediately to Mary. It was easy to find her in the crowd, even when she was surrounded by people who towered over her, like his heart had a homing beacon for hers.

When Leah turned back to their table, she was smiling warmly. "I bet it does feel personal," she said gently. "And I get it. Believe me, I get it," she laughed. "I've known Mary a long time and two things have always been true. One, her mother is overbearing as hell."

"Overbearing is a kind way to describe that," Knox said.

Leah winked in reply, smiling conspiratorially. "And two, no one has ever been good enough for her daughter, not even her daughter."

"How the hell does that work?" Santos asked, so

annoyed he shifted in his seat. Discomfort had been settling into his limbs for long minutes.

Leah shrugged and grabbed a chocolate chip cookie from the plate she'd brought them. "I don't know, man. I'm not a repressed woman of the church struggling with the way my life is compared to what I thought it would be."

"You sound like a therapist," Knox said.

Leah laughed. "No, sir, but I spent enough time on a couch to get the gist *and* I may or may not have been raised by a woman eerily similar."

"Ah, got it," Knox laughed, nodding. "I'm sorry."

"Ooh, don't be sorry. She made me who I am, for better or for worse."

"I like you," Knox said.

Leah beamed. "I like you too. And you," she said, aiming her smile at Santos.

"Same," he ground out.

"Don't mind him," Knox said. "He likes to hold a grudge."

"If grudges looked that good on me, I'd hold 'em too," Leah said.

"I know that's right," Knox said, squeezing Santos's shoulder once more before finally letting him go.

Santos didn't want to smile, but his face did warm under their attention.

"I hope you can salvage the day. It's Christmas Eve, the perfect time to enjoy the company of our loved ones and all that jazz."

"Our loved one is over there," Knox reminded her before Santos had the chance to say it with much less care.

"Okay. Good point," Leah conceded.

Mary was closer now, sitting at a table nearby, nodding along as her mother spoke. Santos could see discomfort clearly written all over her body — her tight smile, clenched jaw, and the way she was bunching the fabric of her dress in her fists under the table. He hated seeing her in distress and hated even more that he didn't feel like there was anything he could do to soothe her.

Not from so far away, at least.

"So why doesn't she like you?" Knox asked Leah.

Leah popped a pretzel into her mouth. "The feeling's very mutual." Knox and Santos chuckled softly. "I'm not good enough for her daughter either."

"She likes Keisha," Santos offered.

Leah rolled her eyes. "I love Keisha, but she's also a repressed, respectable Black woman. I've been trying to break her out of that shell. It hasn't worked yet, but I won't give up on her."

"That's nice of you," Santos deadpanned.

Leah burst into laughter. "Yeah, it's basically what I'm doing to ensure I get into heaven. You know, just in case it's real."

A small laugh fell from Knox's lips.

"I mean she's my friend, I love her, blah blah blah, but also, just in case I end up at the pearly gates, saving my best friend from a sad, small life without sex will count for something."

Knox's laughter only grew. He laughed so hard he had to cover his face with his hands. He laughed so hard it even lifted Santos's mood.

"I like you," Santos said, and Leah winked at him.

It took a few moments for Knox to pull himself

together. In the meantime, Leah grazed off the snack plate she'd ostensibly brought for them.

"Look, I can't tell you how to handle this situation 'cause it is weird as f— It's very weird," Leah said, looking around just in case someone heard her almost curse inside the church. "I love Mary enough to deal with her mother's crappy behavior. It helps that I only ever have to see her once every blue moon. You'll have to decide if you can handle it or not. And for the record, I won't judge you either way." She winked, grabbed a cup of juice, and dove back into the crowd.

"She's quirky," Santos said, and Knox nodded serenely. "We shouldn't have come," he whispered, guilt making his voice hoarse.

Knox turned his body fully toward Santos, spreading his knees so he could scoot closer. His left knee dug into Santos's thigh. The pressure wasn't the same as a hug, which was what Santos wanted, but it was sorely needed.

"You sound like you're worrying again."

Santos nodded and swallowed a lump of emotion. "'Cause this is my fault."

"We don't gotta assign blame. It won't lead us anywhere good. We decided to take this trip together."

"I pushed her into it," Santos countered.

Knox shook his head and leaned on the table, giving them the semblance of privacy. "When have you ever been able to push her into anything but me?" Knox whispered, his gaze hot with desire.

They stared at one another in their silent corner, remembering last night with Mary between them, both of them inside her to the hilt. Every time Knox's dick touched the back of Mary's throat, her pussy contracted around Santos's shaft. Even just thinking about it now made Santos's stomach clench with need.

Knox smirked and sat back in his chair. "We made the decision together," he repeated. "We're here now and we can't take it back, so let's make the most of it."

"How are we going to do that when her mother won't even let us near her?"

Knox opened his mouth but snapped his jaw shut and sat up straight in his chair. Santos followed the line of his gaze and found Mary and her mother finally heading in their direction. He tried to gauge Mary's mood by the tight smile on her mouth, but it was as blank as her face.

Knox and Santos stood politely as they approached.

"Howdy," Knox called in a bright, cheery tone.

"Hello," Santos breathed in a cautious voice. Mary was looking in their direction but not at them and it broke his heart.

Her mother stared at them as if they each had two heads. "Mary says that you...three have plans with a friend tonight and need to leave early." Her voice was tight with a tone Knox couldn't identify.

"We sure do," Santos replied quickly, glancing at his watch. "We should probably get going. Don't want to be late."

Mrs. Woods nodded once before turning to her daughter. "I'll see you tomorrow for dinner." It wasn't a question.

"Yep. Yes, ma'am," Mary replied with thin enthusiasm. "Is dinner still at three?"

"Yes, but I'll need you there by eight at the latest."

Mary didn't flinch, but Santos could feel her stress. "Sounds good."

Her mother stared at her for a few pregnant moments of silence before nodding and walking away without another word.

They watched her retreat into the crowd. As soon as she was out of earshot, Mary swirled around with wide eyes. "Can we go? Please?"

A pit opened in Santos's stomach. Mary didn't beg for anything. Not outside of the bedroom, at least. "Yes," he said softly, his heart wrenching in two.

"Of course," Knox echoed.

They didn't rush from the room, but they didn't dawdle either. Mary waved at people as she left and Santos nodded in Leah's direction as they passed, but he'd never been happier to leave an event before. Mary led the way past the sanctuary, opening her arms wide as if they'd been bound demurely to her sides while in her mother's presence. She tipped her head back and raised her face to the sky, gulping fresh air like a starved woman.

Santos and Knox watched quietly as Mary crawled from the shell she'd been hiding inside for the past hour. By the time they made it to the car, Santos's shoulders still felt heavy, but Mary turned to them, looking like she had a new lease on life.

"Doin' alright, sweetheart?" Knox asked carefully.

"No, but once we get home, we're gonna fuck each other until I can't think anymore," she breathed excitedly. Knox crossed his arms but Mary raised her hands. "Not because I'm running away from my feelings," she added hastily. "But because we just survived that shitty hour not together and I think we should reconnect like a puzzle."

Santos squinted in confusion. "Huh?"

Knox chuckled softly and walked toward her. "She means our pieces in her slot, don't you, sweetheart?"

"All my slots," she whispered, her beautiful mouth curving into a generous smile.

"That's our girl," Knox whispered.

Santos didn't feel light enough to laugh, but he finally felt like they were on the same page. He pressed the button on his key fob to unlock the car doors. "Whatever. Let's get the fuck out of here."

Mary gasped. "Don't curse in front of the church," she said before bursting into happy, relieved peals of laughter.

KNOX

They made it back to Dom's house and flopped onto the couch as if they'd spent an eight-hour workday in a factory rather than an hour at church. Knox had tried to keep his expectations in check, especially because of Mary's trepidation about bringing them home. Now that they'd met her mother and knew what they were working with, Knox was assured that they could weather this storm together, but tonight they needed to rest and recharge. And, of course, reconnect.

"Let's stay in tonight?" he said.

"Yes, oh my god," Mary sighed and closed her eyes, taking in a few deep breaths.

"I'm sorry," Santos said carefully.

He looked like a sad puppy dog and it broke Knox's heart. It also made his dick hard. Feelings were complicated.

She didn't immediately respond, so they watched her until she licked her lips and patted Santos's thigh. "It's not your fault," she finally said. "You didn't know that it would be like this. I hoped it wouldn't, but..." She opened her eyes and stared up at the ceiling. "I always hope she'll be different, but so far, she never is."

Knox grabbed her hand and twined their fingers together. "I don't mean to sound rude, but I'm having a hard time imagining how someone like that raised someone like you."

He'd been thinking about this all day while helping Santos weather the storm of his emotions and holding himself together at the same time. Knox knew a thing or two about the disconnect between parent and child, but Mary was warm, open, and loving; her mother was not.

A ghost of a smile crossed Mary's lips. "When I was little, my great aunt Jeannie was my refuge. She babysat me until I went to school. Whenever my parents had to work late or wanted a date night, they'd drop me off at Jeannie's. I think I take after her." She turned to him with glassy eyes. "She's the most loving person and she curses like a sailor."

"That sounds like you," Santos breathed, turning into her side, tentatively resting his hands on her stomach. When she didn't skirt away from his touch, he wrapped his arms around her waist and held her close, his big, tense body melting into hers.

"Are we gonna meet Jeannie tomorrow?" Knox asked.

Mary's face drooped sadly as she shook her head. "Jeannie moved to Georgia like a decade ago. I stopped coming home for the holidays when she left. It was too hard to be here without her."

Knox nodded. "Maybe we should go to Georgia some time?"

"That would be nice. Anyway, wanna open some Christmas presents?" Her smile caught Knox off guard.

"You alright there, sweetheart?" Knox asked.

She shook her head, dislodging a few tears from her eyes. Knox rubbed them away with his thumb and Santos pressed his face into the crook of her neck. "I will be, though. I just don't want to be sad on Christmas Eve."

"Okay," Knox whispered, trying not to cry himself. "Let's start with mine."

He lifted her hand to his mouth and kissed her skin before jumping up from the couch. Knox rushed into the bedroom and found the bag of presents he'd been lugging around the entire trip. When he came back into the living room, Mary's head was resting on the back of the couch while Santos kissed her throat and chest. Knox could see the imprint of her nipples through her dress from across the room. He hated to interrupt them, but Mary's eyes turned in his direction. There was a dreamy smile on her face as Santos started sucking her nipple through the fabric.

He raised his eyebrows and she licked her lips. "We're ready," she said in that delicious warm honey voice she used when she was horny.

"Clearly. Now break it up," he laughed.

It took a few seconds for Santos to raise his head from her chest, but he managed it eventually. After the last few hours, being alone together felt like heaven and all the tension in their bodies finally started to dissipate.

Knox took a seat on the coffee table facing them. He pulled the first gift from the bag. Knox's wrapping paper was reflective silver. He'd have preferred something with a more traditional Christmas color scheme, but by the time he'd stopped by Mr. and Mrs. Kentish's general store, silver was all they had left. It had taken too long to find the right gifts for each of them because none of them really *needed* anything, but Knox thought he'd finally figured it out.

"I'm not too good at gift wrapping," he breathed apologetically as he handed them an identical package each.

"It shows." Santos muttered.

"Shut up," Mary said, beaming at Knox. "They're cute."

"Nah, they're terrible, but I love you for lying to me. Now open 'em," he said excitedly.

While Santos tried to find a convenient corner to pull the wrapping paper apart, Mary attacked it with a satisfying rip down the middle.

"Oh. My. God," she breathed just as Santos grunted.

"I'm not putting this on," he huffed, vigorously shaking his head.

"Why not?" Knox laughed.

Santos held up the sexy cop Halloween costume Knox had given him as if *that* was the only answer he needed.

"Oh, I'm wearing the fuck out of this," Mary said, holding up her matching sexy baker costume, which was mostly just the tiniest apron imaginable; definitely never passing the health code. He'd driven four hours to the closest Halloween store and seeing the costumes in their hands had his heart racing and his dick hard.

"I don't think it's gonna cover the important bits," she said, licking her lips. "Perfect."

Santos was surprisingly unmoved by Mary's glee as he tried to glare a hole in Knox's head. "There better be one more costume in that damn bag."

Knox reached into the bag before Santos was even done speaking. He'd wrapped this one too so they could share in this moment fully. He ripped his present open and showed them his matching sexy firefighter costume.

Mary's giggles filled the room, softening both of their hearts. Not their dicks, though.

Santos grunted and stood from the couch. "My turn, I guess."

He retrieved his own bag from the bedroom and handed Knox and Mary a small package each. Based on the white snowmen on the red background, Santos had picked up his wrapping paper from the Kentishes' general store earlier than Knox. They were wrapped better than Knox's as well, but just barely. Mary and Knox ripped their presents open at the same time, exposing two small jewelry boxes.

"I'm not really a jewelry kind of person," Knox said, eyeing the box warily.

Mary gasped when she pulled the box open. "It's beautiful."

Knox leaned over, trying to see Mary's gift, but Santos kicked his foot. "You have your own."

Knox pulled the velvet box open nervously and then

smiled at the dog tag with his, Mary's, and Santos's names etched into the metal. He pulled the chain he always wore under his shirt out into the open. Santos mirrored his movements while Mary lifted her dog tag by the chain. Now that it was out in the open, Knox could see that Mary had a delicate necklace instead of the standard issue bead chains they wore.

"Do you have one?" she asked Santos.

Knox watched as he sorted through his Air Force issue tags and found the one that matched theirs. Mary reached forward and ran an index finger over the script.

"This is perfect," Knox said, but then he frowned. "Fuck, I shoulda got better gifts."

Mary grabbed her costume and the chain in her hands and held them to her chest. "Shut up. I love them both. They're exactly like you two," she laughed.

"What does that mean?" Santos asked.

"Playful and meaningful," she said with a smile, pointing at Knox. "Serious and heartfelt." She pointed at Santos. "You two are the perfect pair. For me," she added after a brief pause, the smile lifting her perfectly plump cheeks.

Santos leaned toward her and kissed her temple, but then he rolled his eyes at Knox. "I'll wear the hat and the badge, but that's it."

Knox squinted in confusion. "Are we supposed to be sad about that?"

"That's basically the entire costume anyway," Mary added helpfully.

"What did you get us?" he asked Mary.

She bounced in her seat. "Put my necklace on first." She

pushed the chain into Santos's hands and turned away from him, winking at Knox while he worked.

Mary speed-walked to the bedroom and came back with her arms full of gifts — a few wrapped packages of varying sizes. She handed them off to Knox and Santos and then waited, excitedly bouncing in her seat.

Knox tore his package open with a wary frown that deepened when he saw the object inside. "I don't get it."

When he looked to Santos, the other man had a similarly confused look on his face while he turned the dildo in a box around for Knox to see. They both turned to Mary with eyes full of confusion.

"You realize we have penises, right?" Santos said.

Mary rolled her eyes. "Duh. These are for me." She reached out and grabbed the dildo in Santos's hand and the harness in Knox's.

They stared at her for a second until understanding finally dawned on them. Knox felt sweat collecting on his brow and he couldn't stop the smile from lifting his face.

"My gift to you both," she said with the dirtiest grin, but then it broke into a gleeful smile. "We can wear the costumes!"

Santos groaned and dropped his head into his hands. "What the fuck am I going to do with you two?"

Mary leaned over and pressed a kiss to his temple. "You already know," she whispered, winking at Knox again.

They were all so tired, but the night was young and there was no rush. They moved to the bedroom surrounded by gleeful laughter and kisses, happy to be right where they belonged.

HAPPY HOLIDAYS FROM SEA PORT

Christmas Day

MARY

They wanted to sleep in, but they couldn't. If she were home alone, Mary might've pretended to oversleep if only to shave off an hour or two of her mother's nitpicking, but Knox and Santos hated being late. A few minutes before eight, they climbed from their car, silent, sleepy, and stressed. Her mother texted a grocery list first thing in the morning. No greeting, no holiday emojis, just a couple more sweet potatoes and eggs and whatever else she was running low on before dawn. The only good thing about having to go to the grocery store was having Santos and Knox there to carry her bags, at least.

Mary did all the driving since she could still navigate her hometown even when half her brain was asleep. She had to circle the block a couple times before she found an open parking spot three blocks away. The walk was bearable, but the wind slapped them in the face as they made their way to Mary's childhood home.

"Bug, is that you? Bug!"

Mary froze at the sound of her nickname. She hadn't heard that name in person in years and it confused her sleepy brain for a few seconds. Her feet stopped moving and sleepy Santos walked straight into her back.

"Sorry," he grumbled.

"Bug?" Knox breathed.

She searched for that voice in the quiet neighborhood, scanning the neighbors' lawns for some reason. Finally, a black car pulled up along the curb and her cousin Lamar popped out of the driver's door.

"Girl, what the hell are you doing here?" he called, waving at her before leaping onto the sidewalk because Lamar was Lamar.

Mary sighed happily. "Hey, Lamar," she waved.

"Your mama didn't say you were home."

Mary took that mental hit in stride; she was used to it. "Well, I'm here," she cried.

"You are!" he cried back, opening his arms and pulling her into a hug.

"You smell great," Mary mumbled into his chest, surrounded by his floral perfume.

"And I look better," he said, stepping back from their embrace to do a little twirl. "See this fashion?" he asked, opening his coat to show off his stylishly cut gray suit for their appreciation.

"So you're still a fool, huh?" Mary laughed.

"'Til the day I die." He lifted his gaze over her head and gasped slightly. "Now who do we have here?"

"What do you mean?" Mary asked, feigning ignorance.

Lamar sucked his teeth. "The two fine men you got

toting your bags," he said, turning his gaze back to Knox and Santos.

Without turning around, Mary motioned toward them with her right hand. "Lamar, this is Knox and Santos. Santos and Knox, this is my cousin Lamar, who wouldn't understand subtlety if it ran him over like a high-speed train."

"Nice to meet you, gentlemen," Lamar said in the softest come-hither voice Mary had ever heard.

Knox leaned around Mary to offer his hand. "Nice to meet you."

Lamar responded with a flirty smirk that carried into Santos's handshake. "And now which one of them is single?" he mock-whispered to Mary, eyeing them suggestively.

"Neither. They're both mine," she said, a proud, possessive smile lifting her face and her mood. Knox and Santos stepped close as if they'd choreographed it beforehand.

Lamar's mouth fell open and he took a couple of steps back. "Two men?" he gasped. "And you're bringing them to your mother's house? For Christmas?"

"I am." Mary smiled, feigning a confidence she desperately wished she felt.

"Does she know?" he whispered.

"She does." It took all of Mary's energy not to let her smile slip. Her empty stomach was trying to tie itself into knots and she was worried the stress might make her throw up as she waited for Lamar to fill the silence.

"Girl, lemme get on to the liquor store right quick. This is gonna be better than that time Rachel brought that married deacon to Easter. You remember that?"

"Her mama threatened to cut him *and* the pastor. How could I forget?"

Lamar nodded sagely. He eyed Knox as if he was still trying to put the puzzle pieces of her relationship together. "But I thought you moved to the middle of nowhere?"

"I did," Mary replied happily. "We met there."

Lamar's eyes widened. "Well, shit, maybe I need to come out there for a visit. These apps are drier than the damn Sahara, and now you coming back here with *two* fine ass men," he muttered to himself, heading back toward his car with a wave over his shoulder. "I'll be back, Bug. Don't let your mama start no shit until I am. And Mary?"

"Yeah?"

Lamar stopped at the driver's door and gave her a soft, genuine smile Mary realized she'd missed something fierce. "You look happy."

"I am," she beamed.

"Good. Happiness looks damn good on you." He slipped into his car and pulled carefully into the street.

"I can't tell if that went well or not," Knox breathed.

Mary turned toward them, feeling awake for the first time all morning. She also felt optimistic for the first time since they left Vegas. "It went very well."

"Bug?" Santos asked, lifting his eyebrows.

Mary was saved from answering that question by her mother's voice. She called to her from the front porch.

"Yes, mama?"

"Get on in here. It's chilly. Don't need you catching a cold." Her mother waved them through the small gate and up the porch. They stopped at the bottom of the steps for her mother to glare down at them. She was in a dark green sweatsuit, her hair still covered in a satin bonnet.

"Good morning, Mrs. Woods," Knox called in a bright

voice. He was probably giving her mother his best smile, but Mary knew it wouldn't matter and it broke her heart.

Her mother's lips pursed together in a frown. "You brought your...friends too?"

Mary clenched her fists at her sides and took a deep breath. "My boyfriends, mama. I brought my boyfriends to Christmas dinner, yes."

"Lower your voice. The neighbors don't need to know all our business."

Mary wanted to yell that this wasn't *their* business, it was *her* business, but she clamped her lips shut and stepped onto the porch. Her mother looked them over one by one, making a small clucking sound in the back of her throat, before she turned and walked into the house without a word.

Knox reached around Mary to hold the screen door open. "It's always gonna be the three of us," he whispered. "Nothing can change that."

She nodded quickly, sparing him a smile before stepping into her childhood home as dread washed over her.

KNOX

"Where's that accent from, young man?" Mary's uncle Pete, who everyone seemed to just call Mister, asked. Knox had been sitting in the living room talking to Mister for over an hour, and this was the third time he'd asked.

"Early-stage dementia," Lamar whispered in explanation.

Knox's frown relaxed and he nodded. "Texas, sir," he told Mister again.

"Oh! Our people are from Georgia," he said. Again. "Lemme top up your drink."

Knox had a flashback to Santos's uncle getting him relentlessly drunk and his stomach lurched. He couldn't do that again, certainly not here; Mrs. Woods wasn't nearly as fun as the Santos family. He didn't want to be rude to Mary's uncle, though, so he held his cup out for Pete to refill with a shaky smile on his mouth.

Mister's drink was a too-sweet punch to hide the bitter bite of cognac; not his favorite, but Mister seemed to love it. Knox glanced at Santos across the living room. He was chatting with one of Mrs. Woods's friends, who'd been introduced as Mary's Aunt Tonisha, nodding as she spoke to him. He spared a quick glance in Knox's direction and tilted his mouth into a small smile.

"There you go," Mister said.

"Thank you," Knox replied politely, pretending to take a sip.

The doorbell rang and Mister turned in that direction. As soon as he looked away, Knox put his red Solo cup on the side table, out of his reach and well out of Mister's sight.

Lamar jumped from his seat and moved to the door as Mary's mother walked into the living room, wiping her hands with a dish towel.

"You're late!" she yelled at the two women who walked inside.

One woman looked to be about in her fifties while the other was maybe a decade older; it was so hard to tell with Black women. What was clear, though, was that these women were related to Mary because they looked like her, maybe even more like Mary than her mother. Although there was a chance Knox only saw the resemblance because they were smiling and happy as they avoided Mrs. Woods's accusation.

"Hey, everybody," the older woman called, handing their bags to Lamar. Pete and Tonisha muttered hello.

"This is Auntie Mickie," Lamar told Knox and Santos, gesturing toward the older woman, "and our cousin Aya."

Knox and Santos stood quickly. "Hello, ma'am," Santos aimed at Mickie.

Mickie eyed them with a smile on her face. "Well now, what fresh blood do we have here?"

Lamar barely stifled a laugh. He'd missed their introduction to Tonisha and Pete so he was reveling getting to see it for himself.

"These are some of Mary's friends from that tiny town she moved to," Mrs. Woods said in a dismissive tone. Knox and Santos cut their eyes at one another.

"Mary?" the younger woman breathed.

"Hey, y'all," Mary said, walking into the living room. She was smiling, but she sounded all wrong to Knox's ears.

"Oh my god!" Mickie and Aya yelled at the same time, rushing around Mrs. Woods to wrap her in a hug, just as Pete and Tonisha had. He wondered how it was possible that everyone was ecstatic to see Mary and shower her with love *except* her own mother, but he couldn't dwell on that right now or else it would show on his face.

Lamar sucked his teeth. "Ms. Rae is a mess," he mumbled under his breath.

Knox returned to his seat next to Lamar. "Who?"

"Ms. Rae. Mary's mother."

"Oh," he said. "I didn't realize that was her name."

"Well, what have you two been calling her?"

"I called her Mrs. Woods this morning. She hasn't said more than a few words to us since we met."

Lamar sucked his teeth louder, shaking his head. "Typical. That woman is set on ruining her relationship with her only child. Some people just refuse to get the hell outta their own way."

Knox caught Santos's eye and frowned at the look of anger and sadness on his face. "Yeah," he breathed. "Sure seems that way."

HAPPY HOLIDAYS FROM SEA PORT

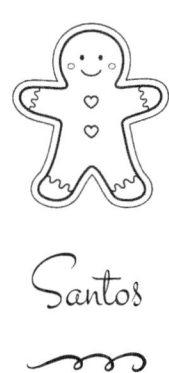

Santos

Santos was the planner in their relationship. Knox was the charm, Mary was the vibes, and Santos brought the detailed route they took from Sea Port to Denver, Vegas, Berkeley, and back again with precision. Santos was the one who made sure their spare tire was inspected before they left, the one who found motels and hotels in their budget, even booking a few early on to make things easier. He tried to account for everything, but he hadn't considered the emotional toil all this would take on them and their relationship. There'd been far too little time to process their feelings and now he felt like an overfilled balloon ready to pop.

If he could go back in time and do it all over again, he would've set an alarm to get up early and go for a morning run to blow off a little — or a lot — of steam. Maybe if he'd done that this morning, he wouldn't have been sitting at Mrs. Woods's dining room table anxious, annoyed, and a little tipsy with a full belly. He'd probably never be able to ask Mary to make her mother's gumbo without remembering how cold she'd been to all of them, especially Mary. So he ate three bowls, figuring this would be the last time he'd ever taste it.

"This really is the best gumbo I've ever had, Mrs. Woods," Knox said again. He'd tried giving Mary's mother this compliment a few times over the course of the meal and she rejected it a new way each time — pretending not to hear, thanking Lamar, and this time with a dismissive grunt. And each time, she seemed to focus a little more of her ire on Mary.

She pointed at the near-empty bowl of rice in the middle of the table. "Mary, go make some more rice, will you?"

It wasn't any more rude or dismissive than every other interaction they'd had with her, but for whatever reason, Santos was at his limit. He dropped his spoon and grabbed the bowl from the center. "I'll do it," he ground out, standing from his chair.

The table froze. Mrs. Woods's eyes lifted from her bowl and finally settled directly on Santos for the first time all day. Her gaze was as unfriendly as Mary's was kind; try as he might, he just couldn't see the resemblance.

"Mary," she said in a brittle voice while staring Santos down, "go make some more rice."

"Yes, mama," Mary whispered, rushing around the table. She brushed the back of Santos's hand and gently pried the bowl from his grasp.

"It's okay," she told him, even though it was anything but.

Santos glared at her mother for a few seconds before turning his eyes on Mary. They had a split second of under-standing before she turned toward the kitchen.

As soon as Santos sat back down, the dinner table conversation picked up again as if that moment never happened. Mary returned after a while with fresh rice for more bowls of gumbo, only to be sent back to the kitchen for more bread and napkins. Dinner moved on, but not for Santos, who abandoned his last bowl of gumbo.

It didn't taste nearly as good anymore.

MARY

B y the time dinner was over and everyone had moved back to the living room for more drinks, Mary was exhausted. She didn't even have the energy to join Mister in a game of dominoes, which used to be their favorite thing to do together. Even if she'd wanted to play, her mother still had her working. Her motivations were obvious — if she kept Mary tied to her hip, she wouldn't get to spend any time with Knox and Santos — and she'd been successful at her mission all day.

Under other circumstances, Mary would've just left or at least gone up to her old bedroom to decompress for a little while like she normally did, but she couldn't leave Santos and Knox alone and she *really* wanted her mother to like them. There was also the matter of her Grampa Earl's cookie.

She knew there was a high probability that her mother

would be on her worst behavior, but she came anyway because Mary wanted — no, needed — Grampa Earl's sugar cookie recipe. Every time she thought about leaving, she admonished herself for giving up so soon. She refused to believe she'd dragged Santos and Knox here and put them all through the emotional wringer for nothing.

Refused.

She'd spent nearly six months trying to recreate the cookie from memory and failed every time. Mary was used to failure, she learned a lesson from every setback, but she couldn't figure out why she was failing and that's what brought her home. The cookies she'd made were fine; they tasted good — great, if she was being honest — but they weren't as good as Grampa Earl's cookies. They didn't melt on her tongue the way she remembered and she wanted the cookies she remembered in her display case. Nothing less would satisfy her or her customers.

Instead of relaxing with a drink in the living room, Mary was helping her mother scrub the kitchen from top to bottom while keeping an eye on the three sweet potato pies in the oven. She was exhausted and desperate to get back to Dom's house and sleep for days, so this was the moment.

Grampa Earl had been terrible about passing his recipes along. He had a habit of giving different measurements to different family members if they even got a recipe at all. More than likely, when someone wanted to learn one of his recipes, he'd subject them to a long, meandering story about his life while he made the dish, like the first baking blogger ever created. Mary thought it was fascinating until years after he died and she realized she'd never taste his sugar cookies again. When Mary shared that sadness with her mother, she'd made a double batch of Grampa Earl's cookies to cheer her up. Mary hung onto those cookies for longer than she should've, not just because they reminded her of her grandfather but because they reminded her that her mother did love her, even if she didn't have the best way of showing it.

She'd asked for this recipe many times before to no avail, but she held out hope that maybe — just maybe — this time would be different.

Her mother was loading a few more plates into the dishwasher when Mary finished sweeping up. She tucked the broom in the corner behind the fridge and took a deep breath.

"Mama," she said in a voice so puny it made her cringe. She wasn't *that* Mary anymore. She cleared her throat. "Mama," she said with a bit more strength this time.

"You getting sick?" her mother asked, closing the dishwasher and moving to the stove to start boxing up leftovers for Mister.

"No, ma'am."

"When you're done in here, go get some vitamin C pills from outta my medicine cabinet. Just in case."

"Okay." Mary learned long ago not to fight her mother about trivial things. It was a trap. She agreed and moved the conversation along. "Mama, I've been thinking about Grampa Earl's sugar cookie recipe."

"What about it?"

"Um, I was wondering if you could...give it to me." The last word squeaked out of her mouth. Her cheeks were hot with embarrassment, but she didn't back down.

Her mother pressed the lid onto the plastic container in her hands and took a slow, tense breath before finally turning to face Mary. "Why do you need that?" she asked in a calm voice that always managed to make Mary feel small.

She'd rehearsed this conversation thousands of times in her head, but dealing with her mother was always unpredictable. She opened her mouth to reply but the words tripped over one another as they fell from her lips.

"Speak clearly," her mother demanded.

Mary pressed her lips shut, took a deep breath into her nose, and let it out of her mouth. "You always said you would teach me how to make them someday and I've been waiting. Also, I'd—" She stopped here to take another breath. "I'd like to make them for my bakery."

"Your what?"

"My bakery, mama. The bakery I own." Mary couldn't hide the frustration in her voice.

For the last year, every time her mother's name popped onto her phone screen, Mary felt forced to shrink herself for the duration of the phone call, avoiding any topic that might lead to a terse fight until eventually, all they had left to discuss was Cat-leen and the bakery. Sure, her mother had never been overly interested in Confections, but she hadn't been rude about it until now.

Her mother scoffed and turned back to packing up the leftovers. "Your grandfather would be turning over in his grave if he saw you right now." That sentence was like a punch straight to Mary's heart — not even her gut. Mary let out a stunned, pained breath. If she noticed the damage she caused, she ignored it. Or maybe she didn't care.

Her mother shook her head and loudly sucked her teeth. "All those sacrifices he made to get you to college. He was so proud when you went to graduate school 'cause you were going to be a *doctor.*" She said that last word like a profanity, as if Mary's entire existence was a stain on the family history. "And what have you got to show for it? A bunch of student loans you can't afford to pay off, no teaching job, a bakery that'll probably fold in a year in this economy, and now you're living in sin with *two* men."

She'd been waiting for this moment, Mary realized. Waiting to unleash a torrent of words strung together only to make Mary feel small. Hell, she probably had a list of all her recent failures ready to lob at her like accusations. Mary had endured a lot from her mother, but somehow, the realization that she'd been waiting all this time to tear her down stung more than the words themselves.

Santos's family had rearranged their entire house to make room for all three of them, sharing their love for Santos with her and Knox. And Ms. Pearl and Marcus had welcomed her and Santos into the warmth of their community because they loved Knox and all people deeply. Meanwhile her mother, the woman who'd given Mary her entire face, had used the same amount of time to get all the ducks of her grievances into a row. It was hateful in a way Mary had just assumed was beneath her mother. And apparently, she was wrong.

Mary wanted to run from the kitchen and cry in the bathroom as she had dozens of times before, but a sound from the dining room caught her attention. Her eyes shifted from her mother's profile to the doorway where Santos and Knox were standing off to the side, hidden from her mother's view. Their faces were pinched with anger, sadness, and frustration. Her mother's grievances stung but the pain on their faces hurt the most. It was one thing to treat her poorly, but Knox and Santos didn't deserve this, and that was a clarifying realization for Mary. Her mother's words weren't gospel and they didn't define her or her life.

And most importantly, she didn't have to stay here and take it.

Her gaze moved back to her mother. "So, you won't give me the recipe?"

She stacked the containers of Mister's leftovers one on top of the other before turning to Mary with a weary look etched into her softly wrinkled face. "I'll give you my daddy's cookie recipe when I see you're living your life right. And you can start by moving home."

"No," Mary said, tripping over her mother's final words.

"Excuse me?"

"I said no, mama. I'm not moving home. I'm living just fine where I am. And if you think I'd give up the life I've built in Sea Port for a recipe, you don't know me at all."

Those words didn't go over well, but Mary felt freer by the end. So goddamn free.

"We'll see," she said, snatching Mister's leftovers from the counter. "Tomorrow I want to take you by Tonisha's house. Some of the church elders will be there and they want to see you again since you haven't been home for so long." She pulled the refrigerator door open with far more force than was necessary. "Just you," her mother clarified. "You can leave your friends at Dominique's."

Mary's anger burned away the fresh wave of triumph. "They're my boyfriends, mama, and I'm not leaving them at Dom's. If you want me to come tomorrow, they come with me." And then it was her turn to put her hands on her hips. "And we'll introduce them as my partners."

"Girl, if you don't put your hands down," her mother warned. "And you ain't bringing those men to meet the deacons. Not at all."

"Then I guess I'm not going." Mary shrugged, hands still on her hips.

"I'll be by Dominique's tomorrow at ten on the dot. Be ready. And put on something more respectable than that." She ducked down to place the containers in the fridge.

Mary had lived her entire life in the shade of her mother's judgment, always hoping things would improve. Now she knew they wouldn't — she wouldn't. There was no changing her mother, so why bother?

"We're leaving tomorrow morning, mama," Mary said testily.

She pushed the fridge closed and for the first time since they arrived, the wall her mother put between them cracked. "Tomorrow? You just got here."

"And look how you've treated me since," Mary said in a tight, strained voice.

"How have I treated you?" she asked, feigning ignorance.

"Like someone you hate," Mary said, finally admitting the thing that had been sitting at the back of her brain long before she ever even met Santos and Knox. "But I don't hate you. I don't like you too much right now, but I respect you as my mother. And if I stay any longer, I'm gonna say something to you that would betray that respect, so I'm gonna leave. *We're* gonna leave and go back to our life. A life you've made it very clear you don't want to be a part of."

Mary stepped around her mother. She couldn't see Santos and Knox, but she knew they were close by.

"Next time you come home—" her mother called to her, but Mary cut her off and turned with a sigh.

"I'm not coming home again, mama. Not to see you, at least. Why would I?"

Her mother pressed her lips together for a second. "Is that a threat?"

Mary shook her head sadly. "No, ma'am. You raised me better than that. But it is a promise. I'm gonna go back to Sea Port and get on with my life. A life that I'm spending with the two men you've barely acknowledged all day. Eventually, we're gonna have kids — your *only* grandchildren — and you're never gonna meet them."

Mary's mother frowned but didn't speak.

"I'd love for this not to be the case, but we can't make a relationship work if I'm the only one trying. If I'm the only one who cares. I might've tolerated you treating me like this before because I didn't know any better or I thought you would change, but I'm not gonna subject Knox, Santos, and any future tall, big-headed kids we have to it. Merry Christmas. Goodbye."

Mary turned on her heel and walked through the dining room into the living room, where she found Knox and Santos standing at the front door, their arms filled with all their coats and Mary's purse. She held herself together long enough to hug her aunts, uncle, and cousins. She promised Lamar she'd stay in better touch and tell him when a gay millionaire bachelor showed up in Sea Port. She felt close to throwing up. She even let her Aunt Mickie and Aya hug her tighter than normal like they always did, as if their embraces would make up for her mother's treatment. It didn't, but she appreciated the effort all the same.

Before she left, Mary pulled a wrapped present from her purse and handed it to Mickie. "For mama," she whispered before leaving her mother's house for the last time. Then she crawled into the back seat of their car with Knox and cried her eyes shut while Santos drove them back to Dom's.

Merry fucking Christmas.

HAPPY HOLIDAYS FROM SEA PORT

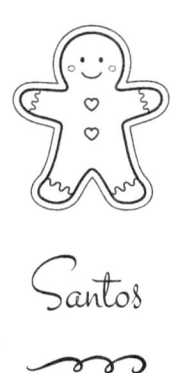

Santos

If Santos had his way, they would've left that night, but Mary fell asleep curled in Knox's arms, so he left her at peace even though he wasn't. Knox held her and eventually drifted off to sleep while Santos channeled his hurt and anxiety into packing their suitcases, even though there was a chance Mary would change her mind when she woke up.

She didn't.

By the time Santos woke, Mary was sitting at Dominique's kitchen table writing a thank you note while Knox packed their car. They made breakfast while Santos showered and they were on the road before the sun had fully burned away the early morning fog. Knox and Santos shared the driving duties while Mary lay in the back seat, silent but for the occasional sniffle. Without the circuitous route to visit their families, they were close to home in just a handful of days, almost as if the universe wanted to get them home as much as they wanted to be there. They stopped overnight in

New Mexico and then again in Tennessee, just to give their car and bodies a rest. The hours sped by in an unconscious blink of an eye but Mary's pain lingered like an extra passenger.

No matter how small or lumpy their beds, Mary crawled between them and cried herself to sleep and no one complained. Back pain seemed trivial next to the hurt they were lugging back from California.

Somewhere in Oklahoma, while Mary was dozing fitfully in the back seat, Knox had the idea to go to Georgia. They could've bypassed the state entirely and arrived back in Sea Port a day earlier, but Mary's aunt Jeannie lived there and he didn't want their trip to end on a sour note. As much as they all wanted to be home, Santos worried that if they returned to Sea Port without any real resolution, the sadness would seep into the nooks and crannies of their relationship and rot.

If they let their trip end like this, Santos worried nothing would ever be the same between them.

It took a carefully executed heist of Mary's phone to get Leah's phone number. One text message asking Jeannie's address grew into a group message that included Keisha, Dominique — even though they'd never met her — Aya, and Lamar before they got the address they needed. Mary was too distraught — or too numb — to notice their route had changed.

It didn't feel like Christmas in Georgia, not to Santos at least. Sure, there was a chill in the air and the sky was gray, but as he eased their car down the long dirt pathway lined by tall walnut trees on either side, it almost felt like spring. But there were festive garlands strung around every other tree and they made Santos smile. The driveway ended at a two-story cottage set in the middle of a large rural property well outside Metro Atlanta. He parked cautiously in front of the house and peered through the front windshield.

"This it?" Knox asked.

"How the hell would I know?" Santos huffed.

The front door opened and an older woman stepped onto the broad wraparound porch. She was average height with medium brown skin, a short salt-and-pepper afro, and a frown on her face that was as much a warning as the shotgun in her hand.

"Well, damn," Knox sighed.

Santos and Knox crawled carefully from the car.

"Hello, ma'am," Knox called out, his hands clearly visible. Santos followed his lead, even forcing a smile on his lips.

"And who the hell are you?" she yelled back.

Santos was about to respond when Mary's dry, cracked voice cut into the silence.

"Jeannie Mae?" She crawled from their car on shaky legs, her eyes bloodshot and puffy. "Jeannie Mae, is that you?"

Mary's great aunt set her shotgun against the railing and stepped onto the top stair. "Bug?" She raised a hand to shade her eyes as a broad smile spread across her mouth. "Girl, what the hell are you doing here?" she asked, breaking out into a peal of bright laughter.

Mary walked toward the house with quick, happy steps.

Jeannie walked back to the front door and called inside. "Esther, guess who's here? Bugsy!" she yelled loud enough for them to hear as they followed Mary up the steps.

"Bugsy?" Santos breathed, furrowing his eyebrows at Knox. The other man laughed with a shrug.

Mary jogged up the last few steps and straight into her Great Aunt's arms.

Santos and Knox stopped a few steps down so Mary could have a moment of privacy. The screen door opened and another woman, this one taller and rail thin with two gray cornrows falling over her shoulders, stepped outside.

"What'd your mama do now?" Jeannie Mae whispered lovingly, confirming that this detour was the right decision. She pulled back to look at Mary, her bony hands wiping Mary's tears away. "Oh, you always did let her get right up under your skin."

"She's her mama," Esther said. "So are these your friends, Bug? The ones Mickie told us about?"

"They're not my friends, Aunt Esther," Mary said in a shaky voice.

"Oh, we know," Esther laughed. "They've been calling me and Jeannie *friends* for close to fifty years."

"Well," Jeannie hedged, "we better be friends to spend all this time together."

"Bugsy?" Santos asked because he couldn't stop himself.

"They nicknamed me Bugsy Siegel," Mary said with a pained sigh.

"Why?" Knox asked.

Jeannie and Esther chuckled loudly. "Because if you had anything sweet on you, Bug here would know," Jeannie replied with a look of pride on her face.

"And she'd shake you right on down for her share," Esther added, running a gentle hand over Mary's hair. "Ain't that right?"

"I plead the fifth," Mary whispered.

"Well now, if you don't want us to call you Bug..." Jeannie said, her own eyes wet with tears.

"It's not that," Mary said. "It's Grampa Earl's cookies."

"What about 'em?" Esther asked. "They're not that bad."

"They're not bad at all," Jeannie said, glaring at Esther. "Last time I made a batch, I didn't even get one crumb 'cause you ate 'em all."

Mary turned around and they glanced at one another.

"You know how to make the sugar cookies?" Santos asked carefully.

"Well, of course, I do." Jeannie frowned. "My daddy taught all his kids how to make 'em. It's only 'cause I'm nice that I let y'all name those cookies after my brother." She rolled her eyes. "God rest his soul. As if he could bake anything else."

Mary's mouth fell open.

"Lovely as this little reunion is, I'm cold. Come on inside. I got some whiskey we can get into."

Mary happily let her aunts shepherd her inside.

"Cold," Santos echoed with a shake of his head. It had to be at least thirty degrees warmer here than it had been in Denver.

Knox rubbed his thumb along Santos's cheek. "Georgia cold. Everywhere can't be Denver."

Santos leaned into his touch. "A shame," he laughed, feeling relaxed for the first time in days.

MARY

"You want it to be crumbly," Jeannie said, burying her hands wrist-deep in cookie dough.

Santos was in the backyard with Esther, Jeannie Mae's wife, shaking pecans from the trees on the large, tranquil property. Knox had refused to go back outside in the cold, preferring instead to relax in the warm kitchen with a strong cup of coffee, watching Mary and Jeannie Mae work.

"I always thought it needed to be wetter," Mary said, inspecting a small ball of dough. "Every time I've tried to make these cookies they've been okay, but not right."

"That's 'cause you need it to be dry, just barely pulled together, and then you gotta let it rest."

"Oh," Mary breathed. "Maybe I overworked it."

"You coulda," Jeannie nodded without an ounce of judgment in her voice. "It happens. If you do that, just throw it in the fridge and forget about it for a little while. They might not be as soft once you bake 'em, but they also might. But you wanna do your best not to overwork all that butter."

"Okay," Mary nodded. "How long should I let it rest?"

"At least an hour, but if I'm lazy I'll let 'em marinate for a day."

"Marinate," Knox chuckled.

"You know what I mean," Jeannie said.

"He doesn't, actually," Mary said, winking at him.

"Anyway, once they're rested, you wanna roll 'em out, get 'em in the oven, and when all that butter melts, you get cookies soft as pillows. At least that's what my daddy used to say."

"Your daddy?" Mary asked in wonder.

"Yes, my daddy. You really thought your granddaddy came up with this recipe on his own?"

"I really did."

Jeannie sucked her teeth. "Just like that man to take the credit."

"So your daddy came up with the recipe?"

"He sure didn't," Jeannie laughed.

Mary stopped working her portion of dough. "Well, then who did, Aunt Jeannie?"

"My daddy's grandmother," she said and then corrected herself, "we think."

"You mean you don't even know?"

Jeannie smiled as she scooped Mary's portion of the dough into her own. "Our people passed down so much from slavery and we've lost a lot of it along the way. We're lucky we even remember the recipes enough to pass them down."

"Yes, ma'am," Mary said, ducking her head.

"And this is how we remember, me teaching you. Something else my daddy used to say. These cookies have been passed down in our family for seven generations. Eight generations now," she said, looking at Mary with eyes full of love.

"Yes, ma'am," Mary replied softly, beaming at her aunt.

Jeannie sectioned the dough in front of them into two pieces and then four. "Let's do an experiment."

"Oh, Jeannie," Mary whined, rolling her eyes playfully.

Jeannie laughed, shaking her head. "If you wanna learn a lesson, gotta learn it well. We'll put these in the icebox for an hour, a couple hours, and overnight to compare."

Mary sighed audibly and Knox smiled, imagining her as a young girl under Jeannie's tutelage.

"But we'll bake these right now," Jeannie laughed. "Can't have y'all driving all the way out here for nothing."

"This wasn't for nothing," Mary said earnestly, smiling at Jeannie with her entire face. "I didn't know you even knew how to make them. I thought only mama did now that Grampa Earl is gone."

"Is that why you never asked me? That's why you went home instead of coming here?"

"That wasn't the only reason," Mary said, her eyes flitting to Knox and then back again. He was watching her with a keen eye and a gentle smile on his mouth. "I just always thought mama would—" Her voice cut off as the pressure of tears built behind her eyes again. Knox sat forward in his chair.

Jeannie tsk-ed and shook her head. "What did I tell you when you called me crying 'cause your mama was mad you applied to out-of-state colleges?" she asked in a patient voice while her hands worked the dough into loose balls and wrapped them in plastic.

A tear fell down Mary's cheek and she wiped it onto her shoulder. "You told me she was worried about the cost, but she didn't know how to tell me that."

"And what did I tell you when she asked if you were sure you wanted to get a PhD?"

"You said she was worried that I wouldn't like it, not that I'd fail, but she didn't know how to tell me that either."

Jeannie hummed her approval at Mary's recall. "Now I'm not making excuses for your mother, but her mother was hard on her just like she's hard on you. Her mama loved her, but that don't mean she treated her right. Sound familiar?"

"Yes, ma'am."

"I don't think a woman who can't tell you she's afraid for you is going to have the patience to teach you how to make these cookies."

"I guess not," Mary said sadly.

"But you got me, and now," Jeannie said triumphantly, "you've got these cookies. Let's get these in the fridge to rest for a bit."

After the dough was put away and the first batch was in the oven, Mary joined Jeannie at the sink and they washed their hands together. "Now why don't you tell me about these boys you're seeing?" she said, glancing across the kitchen to Knox.

When Mary looked his way, Knox was hiding his smile behind his coffee mug, but then he winked and Jeannie burst into laughter.

"Oh, this one's a flirt. Don't you wink at me like that, boy. I'm too old for you."

"I don't know," Knox said. "You look pretty good for your age."

"You don't even know how old I am," she laughed.

"And I'm not gon' ask."

She nodded and turned to Mary. "Mmhmm. He's nothing but trouble, I bet."

"The good kind of trouble," Mary said, smiling so much her cheeks were starting to hurt.

The back door opened and Esther walked inside, followed closely by Santos with a basket full of pecans in his arms.

"Got enough to send Bug home with more pecans than she can use and still make a few pies for the church," Esther said, stripping off her coat in the little mudroom at the back of the kitchen. She hung it on the rack by the door and grabbed the basket from Santos.

"It's going to be pecan season in Confections," Mary cheered.

"You know you could come here and get all the pecans you need whenever you want," Esther said. "How long is the drive from here to Sea Crest?"

"Sea View," Jeannie corrected in exasperation.

"Sea Port," Knox, Santos, and Mary said together.

The kitchen went quiet and Jeannie shrugged. "Never heard of it."

"It's about seven hours," Knox offered, moving the conversation along.

"Oh, that's not bad at all," Esther said. "Y'all could come up here, spend the weekend, and take some of these pecans off our hands. We're getting too old to handle all these trees anyway. And since you have *two*" — she dropped her head to look from Santos to Knox — "big, young, strapping men to help us..."

"That's my overachieving girl," Jeannie whispered. "And

you know, if you spend a little more time here, I can teach you a few more recipes."

"There are more?" Mary chirped.

"Of course, there are."

Mary nodded excitedly, trying to contain herself. "I think we could make that work."

"Good," Jeannie said, offering Mary a paper towel to dry her hands.

"How long until them cookies are done?" Esther asked.

"We got the first batch in now. It'll be about fifteen minutes or so," Jeannie said.

"First batch?"

"We're doing a little experiment," Jeannie said without further explanation, but Esther knew Jeannie and Mary well enough.

"So I guess you're spending the night?" she asked, failing to hide her own excitement.

"If that's alright with you two," Mary said.

"Of course, it's alright. Don't nobody come out here to visit us," Esther said.

"Is that okay with you two?" Jeannie asked Knox and Santos.

"Depends," Knox said. "You gone make me go out and pick pecans too?"

Esther gave him a charming, toothy smile. "Sure am."

"Then it's alright with us," Santos answered quickly, a wicked smile on his face aimed directly at Knox.

"Good," Jeannie cut in. "We can have a couple cookies for breakfast."

Esther rolled her eyes. "This family and these damn cookies."

Knox couldn't help but laugh as Esther ambled out of the kitchen.

"They're the best cookies," Mary assured them.

"I believe you," Santos said, brushing his mouth against Mary's cheek.

"Oh, and he's the pushover," Jeannie cried in understanding.

"I'm not a pushover," Santos replied quickly, affronted.

"The hell you aren't," Knox laughed.

"Watch your mouth, young man."

Knox stopped laughing and sat up straight. "Yes, ma'am. I apologize."

"Oh, don't listen to her," Esther laughed, walking back into the kitchen with a bottle of whiskey and tumblers for each of them in her hands. "She curses like a sailor every day of the week except Sunday."

"Well, it's Sunday now, ain't it?" Jeannie asked, irritated.

"And it's just past noon," Esther said. "Time for a little drink."

HAPPY HOLIDAYS FROM SEA PORT

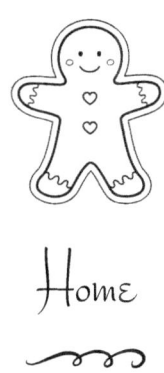

Home

MARY

Mary felt like herself again. She wasn't the same person she'd been when they left Sea Port, but she also wasn't the shrinking violet her mother had cowed into submission on Christmas Eve either. Under her aunts' tender attention, Mary started to crawl out from her shell, becoming the woman Knox and Santos loved again.

The version of herself she loved.

It was well before dawn and the house was quiet in a way she only ever heard out in the country. It reminded them all of Sea Port and their little house on Perv Place. They'd decided to spend a few days with Mary's great aunts so they could end their trip on a peaceful note, but it was almost time to leave for real.

"I miss Cat-leen," Mary whispered.

They were lying in bed, bodies crushed together, staring at the ceiling in the dark. The king-sized bed in Jeannie and Esther's guest room felt like a luxury after weeks of travel stress, especially because it was on the other side of the house from their master suite. Privacy was heavenly.

"'Cause y'all grown," Esther had said with a wink that exasperated Mary and Jeannie but made Santos and Knox laugh. They liked Jeannie, but they really liked Esther, and the feelings were mutual.

"I miss her too," Santos said. "Especially her yelling at me to give her food."

"She never yells at me," Knox teased.

Mary turned onto her elbow and looked down at Knox's face. "This is one of those moments where you annoy me."

He lifted his head and kissed her lips. "You're just saying that 'cause you ain't had any coffee yet. I won't hold it against you."

She rolled her eyes but dipped her head to press her smile against his lips. She kissed him slowly, the tip of her tongue playing with the tip of his.

"I'm sorry we convinced you to come on this trip," Santos whispered.

Mary and Knox turned, their cheeks touching as they stared at him.

"This was my idea, but I shouldn't have pushed."

"It was a good trip," Mary whispered. Knox wrapped his arms around her back and pulled her on top of him. "Your parents love me and my womb," she teased Santos.

He turned on his side to face them, scooting into the space Mary left.

"And Ms. Pearl thinks we're good enough for her precious Billy," Mary giggled.

"Let's not get into the habit of calling me that," Knox sighed.

"And even though my mom was...herself, my friends and the rest of my family think you're great. They're gonna be gossiping about you two *at least* until the Fourth of July if Lamar has anything to say about it." Her voice got stronger as she spoke. Knox's calm heartbeat thumping against her chest was beautiful and healing. "I don't want to let one bad thing overshadow all the other beautiful parts of our trip," she said, cupping Santos's cheek. "Even if that one thing is my mother."

Santos wrapped his arm around Mary's waist, pressing his body against theirs.

"You sure?" Knox asked carefully.

Mary chewed the inside of her cheek as she considered the question in depth, but the answer was clear as day. "I mean it. It was well past time for us to meet each other's families. This isn't a movie. This is real life. And in real life, sometimes families suck."

"Not all of your family," Knox amended.

Mary pressed her smile against his again. "Not my entire family," she agreed.

"Although," Santos said, moving his hand over her ass and between her legs. "There might be a few people ready to riot if we don't start having kids like a month ago."

Mary moaned as his fingers dipped inside her for a few seconds before sliding down. Knox grunted, betraying the destination of Santos's hand as his forearm brushed her clit. Santos pulled Knox's shaft from his boxers.

"I'm still on the pill, you know," she sighed, spreading her legs.

"I know," Santos said, lifting onto his elbow. He kissed

the side of her left breast while he moved the head of Knox's dick to her opening.

Mary whimpered and lifted onto her knees for a second before she sank down onto Knox's length. Knox grunted as Santos's tongue circled Mary's nipple, his fingers rubbing the space where Knox's shaft disappeared inside her.

"Fuck," Mary breathed, rocking along his shaft.

Santos laid back on the bed and brought his fingers to his mouth. He tasted them before shoving his hand in his pajama pants.

"When they ask about grandkids, we can tell them we're trying without it being a lie," Santos moaned, stroking himself.

"Fuck," Mary moaned. "Lemme see."

Santos smirked and pushed his pants over his hips so they could watch his dick harden.

"Smart," Knox grunted, jutting his hips up into her.

They stayed like that for a serene, slow moment, Mary and Knox grinding together while Santos got ready.

"Sit up," Knox grunted, his fingers circling Mary's clit.

It took Santos a few seconds to understand Knox was speaking to him and when he did, he scrambled up, pressing his back against the headboard in eager anticipation.

Mary was horny most mornings, but watching Santos and Knox contort their bodies so Knox could swallow half the length of his shaft pushed her past horny until an all-consuming need was burning through her.

She didn't need Christmas presents when she had them. They were the best gift she'd ever received.

It might not have been the life her mother wanted for

her, but this was more than the life Mary wanted for herself; one full of love and happiness and sweet treats.

HAPPY HOLIDAYS FROM SEA PORT

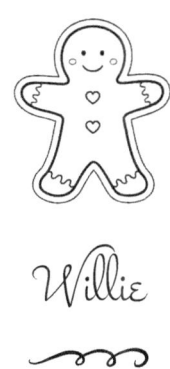

Willie

W illie had been mayor just over three years and today was only the fourth mental health day she'd taken.

It wasn't even an entire day; she just wanted to sleep in, so she did. She woke up just before sunrise, sent a few quick emails from her phone to clear her schedule before lunch, went downstairs to make a cup of tea, and then crawled back into bed with her e-reader and her favorite sex toy.

This used to be her favorite way to spend a lazy morning: rumpled sheets, hot tea, the muffled buzzing of a toy slipping through her folds, and overheated skin.

Gentle, spicy cologne.

She hadn't smelled that cologne in years. She couldn't even find it on this side of the pond — she'd looked — but whenever she scalded her tongue on too-hot tea while teasing her clit, she couldn't help but remember all those mornings they'd spent together.

This morning was good, but lazy mornings had never been the same without him.

It wouldn't happen, but if Danny were standing in front of her, Willie wasn't sure if she'd have the cheek to tell him how much she missed him. That no matter how hard she tried, or which toy she used, or even if she used her fingers, her orgasms alone were never as good as the ones he gave her. That was too vulnerable a position to put herself in when she was the one who left.

It took forever to climax by herself. She could get close, she could get her heart racing, she could get herself wet, but coming was harder than it should've been. Harder than it had ever been with Danny. The only way she could manage to get herself over the edge was when she burrowed under the sheets, closed her eyes, and pretended her toy was his head between her legs. Willie had never experienced a stronger orgasm than when Danny used his mouth and one of her toys to make her squirt. It was filthy and lovely and she missed those mornings almost as much as she missed his smile.

She turned onto her side and curled into a ball, both hands trapped between her thighs. She fucked herself slow and deep, no vibration yet, just the pleasure of feeling full — even if it wasn't as good as the real thing. She used her other hand to rub circles over her clit, while muffling her moans in the pillows.

He used to throw the covers off their bodies so they could lock eyes while he sucked on her clit, for hours if schedules permitted.

A flash of half his eyes smiling up at her while he licked her to orgasm pushed her close. Her heart tapped a jazzy beat against her chest and the memory of the only man she'd ever loved made her legs start to shake.

She could taste the release on the tip of her tongue, which meant, of course, that this was the moment her phone rang. She'd had so little time off recently that she'd forgotten to silence it. Lesson learned.

"Fuck," she groaned into her pillow, and not for the reason she wanted.

She left her toy buried inside her pussy — a silent promise that this wasn't over — and reached for her phone.

"What?" she hissed.

"Well, good morning to you too," Sully laughed, always unfazed by Willie's changing moods.

"I'm taking the morning off."

"Oh, good idea. You deserve it."

"What do you want?" Willie whined, sitting up in bed.

"Can't I just call to say hey?" Sully asked.

"You can, but you don't. What's wrong? It's not... Is everything alright?" She'd almost asked after Bria but immediately started second-guessing herself. It already felt weird talking to her best friend with a dildo inside her, but honestly, weirder things had happened — they were best friends after all. Mentioning Bria in any context, let alone this one, was still weird, though — they were sisters but still strangers — so she let the sentence die.

"So long story short, Lorraine and Jonah lost Mary's cat and we tracked her to your family farm."

"Yes, you have permission to go search my property for her," Willie sighed in frustration and relief. "Okay, bye," she said, trying to rush Sully off the phone. If they hung up immediately, Willie would still have hours of time to masturbate and nap before she needed to be at work.

"Oh, girl, we've been all up and through your property for weeks."

"Weeks? What the fuck?"

"I figured you wouldn't mind."

"I do," Willie said, but she didn't. It was the principle of the matter.

"Now, girl..." Sully breathed.

"Why are you calling me if you've already been trespassing?"

"Whoa, chill out. Trespassing is illegal."

"Glad you realize that even if it didn't stop you," Willie spat back. "Get to the point."

"Rude," Sully said, sucking her teeth. "Anyway, who bought the plot of land next to yours?"

"No one," Willie sighed. She could feel a headache coming on.

"Um, you sure about that?"

"Very," Willie said. "No real estate deals happen in Sea Port without me. Besides, my mom owns that land."

"Um, well, did your mom rent out her farm, then? 'Cause there's a moving truck in the driveway."

"What?"

"I figured you'd want to know, and also I need to know who to ask for permission to let me look for Cat-leen on their property."

"So, hold up. You don't ask me for permission, but you will ask whoever own— My mom," Willie yelled. "My mom owns that land."

"There's no need to raise your voice. Yikes. I'll let you

252

get back to your diddling session. You clearly need the release."

"Oh, fuck you," Willie said.

"We both know it's not me you want to fuck."

"*Don't* go on my mom's property. I'll call her and get back to you."

"Damn, I knew I shouldn't have said anything," Sully mumbled.

Willie sucked her teeth loud enough for her best friend to hear before ending their call.

She pulled the toy from inside herself and stood from the bed, pacing around the room. She found her mother's contact name and pressed the call button for the first time in weeks, then braced herself to hear her voice.

"Well, good morning," her mother trilled as if Willie wasn't actively refusing to speak to her.

"Mama, did you rent out the Freedom Farm?"

"I didn't."

Willie pursed her lips and nodded. "Thought so. Sully called—"

"I sold it," her mother said.

Willie reared back at that as if her mother had slapped her in the face. "What? Why would you sell the family farm?"

She had the gall to laugh. "Why wouldn't I? You're always running 'round town, telling everybody not to hold onto houses new residents could use."

"I mean... Yeah, but—"

Her mother interrupted her again. "Besides, you're my only daughter and you have your father's property. We didn't raise you to hoard land." She stopped here, and the silence between them was heavy; a reminder of why Willie didn't have the energy to talk to her mother right now. "Besides, you always liked the Waltham house better than mine. I thought it made more sense to sell the house to someone else who'll actually use it."

"I-I would have used it," Willie responded in a small voice.

"Oh, honey," her mother whispered, but that was all she said.

"Well, who did you sell it to?" Willie's brain started whirring. Maybe she could buy it back.

"Oh, I don't know. Some foreign corporation."

"Corporation?" Willie cried.

"Well, company. I don't remember the name."

"Mama."

"The business name, I mean. I remember the representative, though. Charming young man. *Very* attractive. Lovely accent. Daniel..." Her mother stopped for a second, clearly trying to recall his surname. Willie's heart had already stopped.

"Joshua. That's his last name. He paid full price. In cash."

"No," Willie whispered, even though every cell in her body was screaming *yes*.

Also by Katrina Jackson

One More Valentine

Heist Holidays

Grand Theft N.Y.E.

The Family

Beautiful and Dirty

The Hitman

The Enforcer

Dolci

The Don

Dolore

Bay Area Blues

Layover

Back in the Day

Curriculum Vitae

Office Hours

Sabbatical

Mosley Coven

The Night Gate (website exclusive)

A Flicker to a Flame

Invocation

-

Standalone stories

Encore

The Tenant

Sex Toy Soldier

Looking

And When You Leave Me

Small Mercies